"When did you get this?"

Becki caught Josh's arm long enough to get a look at the note. "It was in the mailbox when I got here. Courtesy of my sister."

Josh frowned. "Why would she say you don't belong here?"

"Because if I sell, she thinks she'll get more money."

"Who else knew you were moving in today?"

"I don't know." Becki rubbed her worsening headache. "My boss, my roommate, my mom."

"No one from around here?"

"Not that I know of. Like I told my sister, I'm here to stay."

Josh sat beside Becki on the sofa, and her heart jumped at the touch of his knee. "Who else might have sent this note?"

"What do you mean?"

"I mean...who didn't want you moving here badly enough to attack you?"

She dug her fingers into the seat cushion. "You think the note and the incident in the barn are connected?"

Obviously he did. Which meant whoever was slinking around the property had been expecting her.

Books by Sandra Orchard

Love Inspired Suspense

*Deep Cover
*Shades of Truth
*Critical Condition
  Fatal Inheritance

*Undercover Cops

SANDRA ORCHARD

hails from the beautiful countryside of Niagara, Ontario, where inspiration abounds for her romantic-suspense novels—not that she runs into any bad guys, but because her imagination is free to run as wild as her Iditarod-wannabe husky. Sandra lives with her real-life hero husband, who happily provides both romantic and suspense inspiration, as long as it doesn't involve poisons and his dinner. But her truest inspiration comes from the Lord, in the beauty of a sunrise over the field and the whisper of a breeze, in the antics of a killdeer determined to safeguard its nest and the faithfulness of the seasons. She enjoys writing stories that both keep the reader guessing and reveal God's love and faithfulness through the lives of her characters.

Sandra loves to hear from readers and can be reached through her website, or at www.Facebook.com/SandraOrchard or c/o Love Inspired Books, 233 Broadway, Suite 1001, New York, NY 10279.

FATAL
INHERITANCE

SANDRA ORCHARD

 HARLEQUIN® LOVE INSPIRED® SUSPENSE

Recycling programs for this product may not exist in your area.

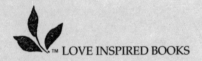 ™ LOVE INSPIRED BOOKS

ISBN-13: 978-0-373-44551-6

FATAL INHERITANCE

Copyright © 2013 by Sandra van den Bogerd

www.LoveInspiredBooks.com

Printed in U.S.A.

You will be consoled when you see their conduct
and their actions, for you will know that
I have done nothing in it without cause.
—*Ezekiel* 14:23

To my stepsister, Rebecca-Becki-Bec,
for letting me borrow all her names.

With special thanks to Karen and Alf Acres for
giving me a ride in their "horseless carriage" and
answering all my antique car questions, along
with Albert Unrau. Also to my wonderful critique
buddies, Eileen, Laurie, Vicki and Wenda, who help
smooth all the story's rough edges. And to the NRP
officers who tirelessly answer my police questions.

ONE

At the sight of her grandparents' old farmhouse, with its wide front porch and empty rocking chairs, Becki Graw blinked back bittersweet tears. All her life she'd longed to live in Serenity's beautiful countryside, but not like this. She stopped at the roadside mailbox and grabbed the mail—a single letter addressed to her. No return address.

That's strange. Who would know to write to her here? She slid her thumb under the flap and pulled out the single typewritten page.

You don't belong here.

Her heart jolted at the cold, black words. Who—

She crushed the note in her fist. *Sarah.* Becki floored the gas and veered into the driveway, then punched her sister's number on her cell phone.

Sarah answered on the first ring.

"You've sunk to new lows," Becki fumed.

"I warned you I'd go to the lawyer if you didn't agree to sell and split everything fifty-fifty. You should've listened to me."

Becki ground to a stop in front of the white two-story willed to her by Gran and Gramps. It wasn't as if they hadn't left her sister anything. She'd gotten most of the liquid assets, not to mention all the financial help when her husband was in law school. Even if Becki sold the house, Sarah probably wouldn't come out that much further ahead.

While Becki would lose the only place that had ever felt like home.

She looked at the darkened windows and empty porch and swallowed a rush of grief. "I'm talking about the note."

"What note? I didn't send any note."

"Right. Because people are lining up to scare me out of here."

To think she'd once idolized her beautiful older sister. No more. At twenty-seven, Becki could finally see Sarah for who she really was—a spoiled trophy wife as materialistic and money-grubbing as her flashy lawyer husband. "Gran and Gramps wanted this house to stay in the family, and I'm here to stay whether you like it or not." Becki punched the power button and jumped from her packed-to-the-roof car.

Inhaling the sweet scent of summer in Ontario's farm country, she shoved Sarah's threats from her mind and turned to the home she loved so dearly.

If only the carbon-monoxide detector had worked the way it was supposed to, Gran and Gramps would be bustling outside to wrap her in their arms this very moment.

Becki scrunched her eyes closed as memories flooded her mind. Swinging from the barn loft into a pile of hay. Fishing in the creek with Gramps. Collecting fragrant bouquets of bouncing bets for Gran. Her summers here had been her happiest. More than once she'd begged to be allowed to live here always.

But not like this—not without them. She pressed her arm against the ache in her chest.

The sun dipped behind the trees with a splash of brilliant reds and purples as if Gramps himself was painting a welcome-home banner across the sky.

I can do this. I want to do this.

Let Sarah call her crazy for quitting her admin job and

giving up the lease on her apartment. So what if she'd never find a husband in the boonies? Maybe she didn't want one. If Sarah's and Mom's unhappy marriage experiences were anything to go by, she was better off single.

Besides, Sarah didn't really care whether Becki found a husband or a decent job in Serenity. All she cared about was squeezing more inheritance out of their grandparents' estate.

Indignant-sounding meows drifted from the weathered hipped-roof barn behind the house.

Kittens! Memories of laughter-filled afternoons playing with each summer's new litter propelled her feet toward the barn. The light was fading fast, but from the way Mama Cat carried on, Becki would have no trouble finding them.

The meowing stopped.

She hurried past the enormous sliding door and pushed through the regular door next to it.

A flight of barn swallows swooped out a hole in the roof.

She paused while her eyes adjusted to the dim light slanting through the gaps in the weathered boards.

A yowl sounded from the back of the barn, but instead of a cat, her gaze lit on Gramps's 1913 Cadillac. *Oh, wow!* How could she have forgotten about Gramps's antique in here?

She drew in a deep breath. Now it was hers, along with everything else at the farm.

Sadness gripped her. Riding in the old car wouldn't be the same without Gramps at the wheel. She just wanted her grandparents back.

She picked her way around the farm implements, her gaze tracking to the car every few seconds. How she'd loved riding with Gran and Gramps, all dressed up in old-fashioned clothes, to the church's anniversary Sunday celebration.

Becki danced her fingers over the hood and marveled at how little dust coated it even after all these weeks. Gramps had always taken such pride in keeping it polished.

A soft mew whispered from the shadows.

Grateful for the distraction, Becki rounded the car. "Here, kitty."

A thunk sounded behind her.

Heart pounding, she whirled on her heel.

A puff of dust floated up from around a block of wood on the floor.

She peered up at the hayloft, thinking a cat must have knocked it down. The dust and smell of moldy hay scratched her lungs.

Movement flashed in her peripheral vision. Something big. Much bigger than a cat.

She ducked behind an upturned wheelbarrow and squinted into the shadows. "Hello." She took a deep breath, forced her voice louder. "Anyone there?"

A faint echo taunted her.

She strained to listen for movement, but she couldn't hear anything over the roar of blood pulsing past her ears. She edged around the wheelbarrow and scanned the other direction.

Something shuffled behind her.

She spun toward the sound. "Who's there?"

A figure lunged out of the shadows, swinging a hunk of wood.

She thrust up her arms.

The wood glanced off and slammed into the side of her head.

White light exploded in her vision. She dropped to her knees, tasting blood. The ground rushed toward her.

Swishing whispered past her ears as blackness swallowed her.

Becki gripped her pounding head. *What happened?*

She opened one eye. The sight of a strange, shadowy room jerked her fully awake. Unfamiliar smells assaulted her. Dirt. And...

She froze. Now she remembered. Gramps's barn. Someone had hit her.

She lifted her head a few inches and waited for the ringing in her ears to subside. She rolled onto her back and peered up at the loft. Was that where he'd been hiding?

Out of nowhere a beam of light flashed over the hood of the car.

She swallowed a scream.

The beam jigged across the barn wall, casting ghoulish shadows.

Hide. She had to hide. Pain rocketed through her head the instant she tried to rise. Gritting her teeth, she dragged herself away from the car—the first place he'd look. Only… why'd he leave, then come back?

She shrank behind an old tractor tire. The reason couldn't be good.

"Bec? You in here?" Joshua Rayne called into his neighbor's barn.

A gasp came from somewhere in the shadows.

He rushed forward. "Bec?"

"Over here."

Josh jerked his flashlight beam toward the tentative response. Bec sat huddled behind a tractor tire, her face chalky-white.

Lowering the beam, he hurried to her. "What happened? Why are you hiding back here?"

"You scared me."

His heart kicked at the crack in her voice. "I'm sorry." He clasped her hand. Her fingers were far more delicate than those of the freckled tomboy she'd been the last time he'd found her hiding in this barn. He tugged her to her feet. "I saw the barn door open and—"

She swayed and clutched her head.

"What's wrong?" He directed his flashlight beam toward her face.

Shielding her eyes, she leaned back against the tractor tire with a moan and soothed her swollen lower lip with the tip of her tongue. "Someone hit me."

"Hit you?" Apparently that car he'd seen hightail it out of the farmer's lane a minute ago hadn't been just a couple of teens looking for a place to park as he'd supposed. He scanned her head for signs of trauma. "Are you okay?"

She pushed his light away. "I will be when you get that out of my eyes."

Josh redirected his flashlight to the floor.

A four-foot length of timber lay on the ground a few feet away.

"Did you see who hit you?"

"I just saw a shadowy figure."

"Tall? Short? Fat? Skinny?"

"I don't know." Bec clutched her head again. "Your average-size shadow."

He needed to get her inside and check her over properly. Irritability could be a sign of a concussion. He quickly swept his flashlight in widening circles. "Why'd you come in here in the dark?"

"I heard cats meowing and hoped to find kittens."

Of course. Same old Becki.

She stepped past him and stroked the hood of her grandfather's old Cadillac. "Then I saw Gramps's car."

At the emotion in her voice, Josh's breath hitched. Her grandfather had had a way of making troubles seem not so bad. The hours he and Josh had spent together tinkering on the "old gal" had been a lifeline after his mother had up and left Serenity without so much as a backward glance. But he couldn't help Josh through this loss.

Josh forced his mind back to the present, to his police

training. "Did you hear or see anything that could help us identify who hit you?"

She started to shake her head, then winced.

Josh resisted the urge to wrap an arm around her shoulders and instead directed his flashlight at the items a thief might have been after. Nothing appeared to be missing, but he couldn't be sure until daylight.

Misty twined herself around his legs, purring. He lifted her into his arms and scratched her chin. "I guess you're looking for your supper, huh?" He turned to Bec, remembering how much she'd adored the cats as a kid. "I've been feeding them since your grandparents..." He lowered Misty to the ground and let the explanation trail off rather than dredge up her loss. He pointed his flashlight at a box beneath the car. "The kittens are under there."

Her delighted squeal tugged a grin to his lips—his first since finding her grandparents' lifeless bodies.

He tugged the box out from under the car.

Bec sat cross-legged on the floor and gathered the kittens into her arms.

Josh chuckled. She hadn't changed a bit. For all her tomboy ways, she was still a soft touch. He gave Misty fresh food and water and then looked around as best he could without leaving Bec in total darkness. If only the barn had overhead lighting, he might find some clue as to who she'd surprised. Most likely kids out for a lark. He hadn't recognized the car he'd spotted as belonging to any of their usual troublemakers. He wished he'd gotten the license plate number.

Josh let his gaze settle back on Bec. Seeing her delight in the wiggling kittens, he could almost feel the years strip away to when they were both kids and life was carefree.

She winced, her forehead creasing.

"Hey, we'd better get you inside. Take a look at that bump. You might need to see a doctor."

A frown curved her lips, but she returned the kittens to the box and pushed it back under the car, which told him more than words would how lousy she felt. When she was a kid, not even promises of chocolate cake and ice cream had been incentive enough to drag her away from the squirming fur balls.

He didn't miss the way she braced her hand on the car fender to pull herself up, either. He moved to her side and, lighting the floor ahead of them, guided her with a light touch to the small of her back. "Do you feel nauseous?"

"A little. But I haven't eaten since lunch."

Outside the barn, he steered her toward his place. "Did you lose consciousness after you were hit?"

"I'm not sure. I think, maybe. Everything went black for a second or two."

"You probably have a concussion. I can do a few tests to see if you should go to the hospital."

She walked a little taller. "I'm fine really. I just need a couple of painkillers. All the doctor's going to do is tell me to go home and take it easy."

"Humor me."

She squinted up at him, then at the tree line that separated their properties and abruptly stopped. "Hey, where are you taking me?"

"To my house. You said you hadn't eaten, right?"

"You don't have to feed me."

"You're in no condition to cook. Besides, it'll be nice to have someone to eat with." Life had been too quiet around here since her grandparents' deaths.

"I don't want to put you out," she protested.

He nudged her forward. "It's no imposition."

She wavered a moment but soon started walking again. "Gramps told me you took over your parents' place after your dad died. Did you still tinker with Gramps on the old car?"

"Yup. Went with them on one of those organized tours they were always taking, too. Saw some cool places most tourists don't get to see."

"I wish I could've gone on one. Gramps said he'd take me when I turned thirteen, but that's when Mom left Dad, and I never got to come back for any more summers."

He steered her around his truck in the driveway. "Yeah, come to think of it, life got pretty quiet around here without you girls."

She swatted him.

He let out an *oomph* and clutched his gut.

"Very funny."

He smiled to himself and mentally ticked off two of his concussion tests. Nothing wrong with Bec's memory or her aim.

He led her to the side of the house and pulled out his key. "Feel like a steak?"

"Yuck."

"You're kidding? You still prefer a burger to steak?"

"Yup."

He pushed open the door, flicked on the light and motioned her in ahead of him. "What a cheap date. Guys must love you."

She squirmed past him into the kitchen, then hesitated, her gaze flagging about, pausing briefly on his Home Is Where the Heart Is plaque, then stealing his way. She looked more uneasy than a suspect in custody.

But unlike with his suspects, he felt strangely sad seeing her this way. "Have a seat at the table while I light the barbecue." He returned a moment later to find her nuzzling his three-legged pooch.

She spluttered at its exuberant kisses and wiped off the slobber with the back of her hand. "What's his name?"

"Tripod."

"I should have guessed. He moves amazingly quick for having only three legs."

Josh filled Tripod's dish, and the pooch demonstrated just

how quick. "While the barbecue heats up, let's take a look at this bump of yours."

She finger combed her hair as if only just realizing how messy it was.

He resisted the urge to tease. Her honey-brown corkscrew curls had always poked out every which way and been peppered with hay or leaves or twigs, depending on where she'd last played.

Dropping her hand, she fidgeted under his perusal. "That bad, huh?"

"I didn't say anything."

She rolled her eyes. "You didn't have to."

He didn't bother to hide his grin. "Show me where you got hit."

She leaned forward and pointed to the back of her head.

He palpated the area. Her hair was incredibly soft and smelled faintly like citrus. "That's some goose egg." He reached into his catchall drawer and pulled out a penlight. "Look at me."

Her shimmering brown eyes turned to him, framed by the longest lashes he'd ever seen. Natural, too.

Her head tilted. "You planning to do something with that light?"

"Patience," he muttered at being caught staring. He flicked the penlight on and flashed it across each eye. "They look good. Equal and reactive."

"Why, thank you, Josh," she drawled, batting those long lashes. "That's the most romantic thing a man's ever said about my eyes."

"What?" He blinked, glimpsed her smirk and gave her a nudge. "You're cute, Bec." He tossed the penlight back into the drawer. "Now, stand up, arms out from your sides, and touch each hand to your nose."

She stood and obeyed his directions effortlessly.

"Okay, take a seat." He opened the cupboard next to the

sink and grabbed a glass and the bottle of painkillers. He tipped two from the bottle, filled the glass with water and handed them to Bec. "Take these, and if you want, you can lie down on the sofa until supper's ready."

She planted her palms on the table and pushed to her feet. "I can't let you cook alone," she protested, then immediately clutched the side of her head.

"As stubborn as ever, I see." He scooped her into his arms and gently lowered her onto the sofa. "Rest. That's an order."

He turned on his heel and did his best to ignore the scent that lingered on his shirt, as it had after their embrace at the funeral home. "I'll get those burgers grilling."

She didn't argue, which worried him. She'd always been a tough kid. Unless she'd changed dramatically in the past fifteen years, whoever had walloped the back of her head had done a serious number on her. Maybe he should ask his sister to come by after her shift at the hospital and check Bec over. It'd be easier than convincing Bec to go there.

He texted Anne a request to stop by and then pulled out the fixings for a decent supper. Sliced potatoes and onions. Peppers, carrots and zucchini for grilling. He dug through the freezer and unburied a couple of burgers that looked more like frozen hockey pucks. Forget it. She could learn to appreciate the good stuff. He tossed the burgers back into the freezer and pulled out a couple of filet mignons.

An hour later, he'd just set the last dish on the table when she meandered to the doorway, rubbing her eyes.

"Dinner is served." He pulled out a chair and waited for her to take a seat. To humor her, he'd put her steak on a hamburger bun and brought out the mustard and ketchup. If she noticed the ruse, she didn't comment.

He took the seat opposite her. "How do you feel now?"

"Hungry. This smells amazing."

He opted to let her nonanswer go. For now. His sister would

be there soon enough. He reached across the table and clasped Bec's hand.

Her eyes widened.

"Let's pray," he said quickly, not sure what to make of her reaction. He bowed his head. "Lord, we pray for Your healing touch on Bec and that You'll comfort her in her grief. Thank You for giving her a safe journey here and for this food and time together. Amen." When Josh lifted his gaze, she was still staring at him, moisture pooling in her eyes.

"What's wrong?"

"No one's prayed for me like that since…Gran and Gramps. I…guess I'd forgotten how nice it felt."

His throat tightened. She'd still have them if only… He gave her hand a warm squeeze. "Let's eat."

They ate in silence for a few minutes, then Bec set down her "burger" and reached for her fork. "What happened to the huge trailer Gramps usually kept the car in?"

"That's over at Pete's Garage. Your grandfather had some trouble with the car during the last tour he and your Gran took, so while we worked on finding the problem, he sent in the trailer to have the bearings repacked. I can give Pete a call. Ask him to bring it by."

"I'm just amazed how clean the car stayed sitting out like that. There wasn't a bird dropping on it."

A steak morsel lodged in Josh's throat. He coughed, swallowed hard. "You mean you didn't pull off the canvas cover?"

"No."

He set down his knife and fork. He'd just assumed… He clenched his fist. *A rookie mistake.* After the front-page article the newspaper had run last week about the Graws, every would-be thief in three counties would've pegged the whole place as easy pickings until the new owner arrived. But if her assailant had come for the car…

"Are you telling me that Gramps didn't leave it uncovered?"

Josh surged to his feet and paced to the window that over-looked the rear of the Graw property. Her arrival wouldn't deter a car thief. He'd have to keep a close watch on the place.

And pray this guy didn't return when Bec was home alone.

Becki shrank into the corner of Josh's couch as he debated with his nurse sister whether she needed to see a doctor.

Even dressed in faded jeans and a black T-shirt, his fur-rowed brow radiating concern, he exuded a powerful pres-ence. Not to mention he'd grown more handsome than ever. His dark hair no longer curled at his temple the way she re-membered, but the trimmed look and broader shoulders re-flected a strength and integrity that had clearly deepened in the past fifteen years.

How cruel could God be to let Joshua Rayne find her cow-ering in the barn as if she was still a twelve-year-old kid?

The kid who'd had a hopeless crush on him—a sixteen-year-old boy who'd had eyes only for her gorgeous older sister.

Not that she'd ever admit to having a crush. Bad enough that she'd tumbled into his arms at the funeral.

Never mind that she'd been a wreck and that when Josh had reached for her hand in the reception line, she'd known, without stopping to think, that *he* understood her sorrow.

She hugged a sofa pillow to her chest. He hadn't hesitated a second before wrapping her in his arms, which should've been her first clue that he was still playing the protective big brother. At the time, she'd barely registered his whispered re-assurances. The grief had been too raw. But now…

She pushed the pillow away. She did not want him thinking she was a helpless female who couldn't take care of herself.

"Can you recite the months of the year in reverse order for me?" his sister asked.

Becki did, then turned back to Josh. "See. I'm fine."

"Concussions can suddenly take a turn for the worse," he

argued, holding out his hand for her car keys. "Can't they, Anne?"

"She's agreed to stay already!" Anne snatched up Becki's car keys and slapped them into Josh's hand. "Go get her suitcase so we can finish the tests in peace." Her eyes were twinkling when she turned back to Becki. "Just humor him for me, okay? I'm getting a free oil change out of the deal."

"No way! He bribed you to stay the night?"

Anne giggled. "Not exactly. I offered…in exchange for the oil change. He would've done it anyway, but this way we set his mind at ease about your condition and I don't have to drive the car back until morning."

"What about your husband? Won't he mind if you don't come home?"

"Not married."

"But…" Becki pointed to the wedding band on Anne's finger.

Anne splayed her fingers and smirked. "That's to keep the doctors and patients from hitting on me."

"You're kidding."

"Nope. Now, stand on one foot, hands on hips, eyes closed, until I say stop."

Becki did as she was told. "I'm surprised Josh hasn't married yet. When I was here as a kid, there was no shortage of girls mooning over him." Her younger self included, but Anne didn't need to know that.

"Yeah, well. He never got over being rejected in favor of life in the big city."

Was Anne talking about Becki's sister? He'd had it bad for her that last summer they were here, and Sarah hadn't discouraged him, even though she was two years older.

"He escaped to the military after that," Anne went on. "Hasn't dated much since coming back. The pickings are slim around here, and he won't dare date a wannabe city girl."

Considering how the city had changed Sarah, Josh was probably smart to hold out for a country girl.

Anne jotted something on her notepad. "Now tell me all the words you can remember from that list I gave you earlier."

Becki repeated them all. "Now do you believe me?"

"How's your headache? Any worse? Feeling dizzy?"

"It still hurts, but no and no."

"All right, yes, I think you'll be fine, but don't tell Josh. It's nice to see him fretting over someone else for a change."

"What do you mean?"

"Um." She bit her lip and glanced toward the door as if he might burst through at any moment. "He'd kill me if I told you."

"We wouldn't want that," Becki drawled, remembering how often her own sister used to preface her secrets with a similar remark. How she missed those days.

"Maybe you could help him stop being so hard on himself," Anne whispered.

"Me?" Becki caught one of her curls, tugging it straight. "Why would he listen to me?"

Becki didn't know what to make of the expression that flitted across Anne's face. Perhaps if she knew her better, but she'd never really met her before today. She'd heard Josh had an older sister, but she'd never been around.

Anne leaned forward and clasped Becki's hand the same way she had when she'd first arrived and expressed her condolences. "Josh feels responsible for your grandparents' deaths."

Becki stiffened.

Anne must have felt it, because she quickly added, "He's not. But your grandfather had complained the day before he died about having a headache, and Josh thinks he should have suspected a carbon-monoxide leak. As if people never get headaches for any other reason!"

Numbness crept over Becki's limbs. "Gramps never got headaches."

"Please don't remind Josh. He's already beating himself up enough over not questioning that. I mean, your grandparents had a carbon-monoxide detector. And it was the middle of summer. Whoever heard of a hot-water tank causing carbon monoxide?"

The screen door slammed shut, and Josh strode into the room.

Becki and Anne sprang apart, but Josh didn't seem to notice. He dropped her suitcase at her feet and waved a note in front of her face. "When did you get this?"

She caught his arm long enough to get a look at the paper. "It was in the mailbox when I got here." She squared her jaw and fought to keep her tone even. "Courtesy of my sister."

He frowned. "Why would she say you don't belong here?"

"Because if I sell, she thinks she'll get more money."

Anne picked up the envelope that had fluttered to the floor. "Where does your sister live?"

"Toronto."

Anne flapped the envelope against her palm. "The stamp on this envelope was never canceled. It looks like someone hand delivered it."

Josh took the envelope from her. "You're right." He passed it to Becki.

So Sarah hadn't been lying. Unless... "She could've asked someone to put it in the mailbox for her."

"Who else knew you were moving in today?"

"I don't know." Becki rubbed her worsening headache. "My boss, my roommate, my mom."

"No one from around here?"

"Not that I know of."

"Could be those developers," Anne chimed in.

"What developers?"

Josh blew out a breath and paced. "A conglomerate of investors who want to see our farmland turned into subdivisions and shopping malls." His scathing tone told her exactly what he thought about their plans. "Have they approached you with an offer to buy?"

"No!" Becki folded her arms over her chest. "Even if they had, I wouldn't sell to *them*."

Josh nodded, his expression grim. "The trouble is you couldn't trust anyone who offered to buy the place not to turn around and pass it on to the developers for a tidy commission."

"Well, like I told my sister, I'm here to stay." Sarah had hated being dumped here every summer. Unlike her big sister, Becki didn't have a life to speak of in the city, and she wouldn't miss it in the least. She happened to like the slower pace of rural living. Maybe she'd even start writing again in her spare time.

"Where will you work?" Anne asked.

"Huh?" Becki shook her sister's voice from her head and focused on Anne. "I haven't figured that out yet. But I'm sure I can find something before my savings run out."

Anne let out a sigh. "Not many new jobs around since the economic downturn."

"Never mind that for now." Josh sat beside Becki on the sofa, and her heart jumped at the touch of his knee. "Who else might have sent this note?"

"What do you mean?"

"I mean…who didn't want you moving here badly enough to attack you?"

She dug her fingers into the seat cushion. "You think the note and incident in the barn are connected?"

Obviously he did. Which meant whoever was slinking around the property had been *expecting* her.

TWO

What would Sarah say if she saw her now, sleeping under Josh's roof?

Well, trying to sleep. Becki flopped over in the unfamiliar bed. Shafts of moonlight shone through the edges of the drapes, highlighting a pair of 4-H trophies perched on the bookcase of Josh's old bedroom.

Her sister would probably feel bad to learn that Josh never got over her. That is…if Sarah was who Anne had meant. Maybe not, since he'd still had a couple of years of high school left after their last summer visit. But he'd sure had it bad for her then.

Becki rolled over and punched the pillow. She didn't want to think of Josh mooning over her sister, especially considering how unreasonable Sarah had been acting lately. Despite her denials, she must've sent that note. Who else?

The two of them were the only living relatives.

Josh was blowing the whole situation way out of proportion. The note and prowler couldn't be connected. She'd probably just surprised a couple of teens who were afraid of getting caught fooling around in Gramps's car. As a cop Josh must see that sort of thing all the time.

But then why was he getting so worked up?

Josh feels responsible for your grandparents' deaths.

Becki's heart clenched. That had to be why Josh wasn't taking any chances.

If only he'd…

She squashed the wishful thinking. If she let her thoughts go there, she'd never get to sleep.

Closing her eyes, she tried not to think at all. An hour later, she was still awake.

A glass of milk might help. She listened for sounds of Anne and Josh still milling about. Hearing none, she pulled on her bathrobe and stole downstairs.

The computer and desk lamp were on in the otherwise darkened living room, but there was no sign of Josh.

She tiptoed to the desk to see what he'd been working on. His internet browser was open to a page about an antique-car theft. Did Josh really think some sort of theft ring had targeted Gramps's car?

She skimmed the article but couldn't see any similarities between that theft and her situation.

A beam of light flashed across the window.

She flicked off the desk lamp and peered past the curtain.

A tall figure disappeared around the corner of the house. Was that Josh?

The kitchen door banged open.

She shrank deeper into the shadows. It had to be Josh. An intruder wouldn't be so noisy. The glow of the computer screen cast eerie shadows on the walls.

Tripod bounded into the room, tongue lolling, followed by Josh, his cell phone pressed to his ear. "Hey, Hunter, can I borrow your game cameras for a couple of weeks?" He walked to the desk and flicked on the lamp. His gaze abruptly veered her way. As his eyes landed on her bare toes, his eyes widened, then quickly traveled up to her flaming cheeks.

"Huh?" He half turned and lowered his voice.

"Yeah, the one with night vision and motion trigger," Josh muttered into the phone. "No, not animals." He pushed back a corner of the curtain and stared out into the deep blackness of the country night. "I'm looking to catch a human."

A human! Becki tugged her bathrobe together more tightly. Why hadn't she stayed in bed?

At least there she could have blissfully deluded herself into imagining there was nothing to be afraid of.

Becki woke early the next morning. She might have let Josh evade her questions last night, but today she intended to get answers. She dressed quickly and tiptoed to the stairs. Halfway down, the aroma of fresh-brewed coffee greeted her, reminding her that *early* had a whole other meaning in farm country. She should've paid more attention to that rooster crowing *before* the crack of dawn.

"Hey, sleepyhead," Anne chirped as Becki meandered into the sunbathed kitchen. Anne handed her a mug of coffee. "How's the head?"

"Good." If she didn't count the gazillion questions that had raced around it all night after overhearing Josh's plan to catch her prowler. "Josh doing chores?"

"They're long done. He only has chickens to feed these days. He's changing my oil. Probably almost done with that, too."

"Will he have to do anything in the fields today?"

"No, he doesn't farm." Anne set a covered platter on the table. "The farmer down the road rents the land."

"But I thought… Josh always talked about running the farm one day."

"Sometimes childhood dreams don't look so rosy when you grow up."

Becki sank into a chair. Her sister had said the same thing. She stiffened her spine. Gran and Gramps's farm was the only place she'd ever felt truly happy. Sure, it wouldn't be the same without them, but she couldn't bear to lose it, too.

"By the time Josh resigned from the military," Anne continued, "Dad had sold off too much of the farm for Josh to make it profitable again."

Becki envisioned him wrestling down a burly drug dealer instead of an ornery cow. "So that's why Josh became a cop?"

"He wanted—"

"To serve and protect," Josh finished for his sister as he strode into the kitchen and plopped a small cage on the counter.

The "criminal" he'd protected them from emitted a tiny peep, and Becki couldn't help but giggle.

"What have you rescued this time?" Anne peered around his shoulder.

He stepped aside, allowing them both to see. A tiny sparrow with a broken wing huddled in a corner of the hamster cage.

"Oh, the poor thing." Becki snagged a piece of toast from the breakfast Anne had spread on the table and sprinkled crumbs into the cage. "Where did you find it?"

Anne rolled her eyes. "The strays always seem to find him."

"What am I supposed to do? Ignore them?"

His sister tipped onto her toes and planted a kiss on Josh's cheek. "Nope, you'd never. That's why I love you."

Josh pulled Anne into a fierce hug, revealing a depth of feeling that caught at Becki's heart. His eyes lifted to hers. More brown than green this morning, they held a warm familial affection that Becki could only dream of now that Gran and Gramps were gone.

Anne ducked out of his arms and grabbed her purse from the counter. "If my car's done, I need to go. Enjoy your breakfast." Anne shook a finger at Becki. "And no heavy lifting. If you get dizzy or your headache persists, have a doctor check you over."

"I will. Thank you."

After seeing his sister out, Josh lifted the lid from a pan of bacon and eggs on the table. "Shall we?"

"Farm-fresh eggs. Mmm. I haven't had a breakfast like this since the last time I visited Gran and Gramps. Your sister outdid herself."

Josh spooned out a plateful of scrambled eggs and bacon. "She likes to stay on my good side so I'll keep her car running."

"I think you'd do it anyway. You always loved to work on cars."

"Shh, don't let her hear you say that." He raised a jug of OJ. "Juice?"

"Uh, sure." Suddenly Becki's insides felt as scrambled as her eggs. To think she was sharing breakfast with Joshua Rayne!

Not only was he more handsome than she remembered; he was as kind as ever. She bet the three-legged dog had been another rescue effort.

She fiddled with her silverware. Obviously the blow to her head had crippled her common sense for her to be thinking up more reasons to still have a crush on the guy. She stabbed at her eggs. It wasn't as if she would ever be anything more to him than another needy stray.

Her mind flailed about for another topic of conversation. "Funny that I don't remember you fussing over animals as a teen. That was more my domain." She struggled to restrain the smile that suddenly tugged at her lips. "Seems to me you were more interested in fussing over my sister."

He choked on his orange juice.

She batted her eyelashes ever so innocently. "Am I wrong?"

He tipped back his head and laughed. "Nothing got by you."

Becki shrugged. "If not for you, I doubt Sarah could have stood being away from the malls for two whole months."

"Not at all like you. You were a farm kid through and through." Amusement danced in Josh's green-brown eyes.

The color reminded her of the grassy meadows she'd loved

to run through as a child. "No. Not like me." She shoveled a forkful of eggs into her mouth and then focused on buttering her toast and the non-Joshua reasons she loved being in Serenity. "If Sarah had her way, I wouldn't stay."

"These old houses can be a lot of work to upkeep."

Her butter knife halted midspread. "You don't think I should stay, either?"

"Not at all. The Becki Graw I remember could do anything she set her mind to."

"Thank you. That hasn't changed. So why don't you tell me about your plan to catch my prowler?"

"Finish up your breakfast, and I'll show you."

Becki finished before Josh and started on the dishes.

"Leave those," he said, tossing the dog his last piece of bacon. "I'll wash them later."

"Nonsense. I've put you out enough."

He reached around her and dropped his plate into the soapy water, his outdoorsy scent teasing her nostrils. "No imposition. I enjoyed the company." He picked up a tea towel and began drying. The graze of his hand as he reached for the mug she'd just rinsed unleashed a flutter of butterflies in her stomach.

Oh, boy. She seriously needed to get over this schoolgirl crush. She'd seen enough failed marriages to know they never lasted.

Marriage? She shook her head. Clearly, no worries there. In Josh's eyes, she was still *little* Becki. She let the water out of the sink and pictured her silly girlhood crush swirling down the drain.

Little Becki grew up a long time ago…the day her parents had announced their divorce.

"Okay, let's go." She dried her hands on the edge of his towel. "Show me what you plan to do with those cameras. I need to start unpacking."

He tossed the towel on the back of the chair and reached

over her head to hold open the door. Tripod raced past and out ahead of them. "I'll carry your boxes into the house."

"No need. I can handle them."

"You heard what my sister said." Josh's stern tone dared her to argue. "No heavy lifting for a few days." He led the way to the barn, where he stopped and scanned the nearby trees. "I'm going to set up a couple of motion-triggered cameras so if your car thief comes back, we'll catch him in the act."

"Then what?"

"I'll arrest him for trespassing and attempted robbery and whatever else I can think of."

"Hmm." She grinned. "Pretty handy having a police officer for a neighbor."

His expression sobered. "No telling what time of day or night this guy might show up. If I'm not around, call nine-one-one and stay locked in the house. Don't try to confront him."

"Don't you think he'd run off if he realized he'd been spotted?"

"Some guys would just as soon shoot a witness as run away."

She planted her hands on her hips. "Are you *trying* to scare me?"

"*Prepare* you." Tripod bounded up to them, barking happily. "Maybe we should get you a dog."

Her heart leaped at the suggestion. "What a great idea. I've always wanted one. Maybe a big lovable golden retriever who—"

"The idea is to get a dog that will scare a robber off, not show him to the silver."

She laughed. "Oh, like Tripod here?"

"Yeah." Josh tousled the scruff on the dog's neck. "He's *not* what you want."

"I like him. He's sweet."

"*Sweet* won't scare away a prowler." Josh rolled open the

barn's big sliding door. "And you definitely have one. I found a couple of footprints." He pointed to the dirt-crusted floor. "See those? Too big for your grandparents or you, and the tread pattern doesn't match anything I wear."

"You were already over here this morning?"

"The sun rises early." He winked.

For the first time she noticed dark shadows under his eyes. Had he even gone to sleep last night?

An hour after she'd headed back up to bed the night before, she'd heard the screen door clap shut and figured he was doing another scan of her grandparents' property. Her property. That trek probably hadn't been the only one.

A cat bolted from the corner of the barn, and Tripod took off after it.

"Won't see him for a while." Josh strode toward the car, which sparkled in the sunlight beaming through the gaps in the boarded walls. "It looks like the guy gave the car a thorough going-over. Both the gear stick and emergency brake lever had been shifted. The toolbox under the seat had been rifled through. Looking for a key, maybe. Best-case scenario, it was a kid playing around." His tone sounded grim.

"But you don't think so?"

He shook his head. "I dusted for fingerprints on the door handles, gear shift and steering wheel. They were clean."

"Clean? As in not even Gramps's prints were on them?" She failed to keep the wobble out of her voice. No prints meant someone had wiped them away.

"Your grandfather was pretty meticulous about keeping it polished. But kids don't usually think to wear gloves. Not in the middle of summer."

She swallowed, forcing calm into her voice this time. "So worst case?" She opened the passenger door, and memories of riding proudly around town with her gramps flooded her thoughts.

"If it's a professional, he's got to realize he wouldn't get far driving this thing out of here before being spotted. So I'm guessing next time, he'll stash a trailer nearby to drive it into."

"You really think someone would go to that much trouble?"

Josh raised an eyebrow. "The last Cadillac of this vintage I saw sell at auction went for eighty-five thousand dollars."

"Are you serious?"

"Trust me." He buffed a smudge from the hood with a fond smile. "If I could have afforded to buy this car from your grandfather, I would have made him an offer."

Becki bit her lip. If Sarah found out what the car was worth, she'd demand it be sold for sure.

Becki's heart lurched at the thought. She didn't care about the money. The car had been Gramps's pride and joy. How could she let it go?

She had sat for hours on the backseat with her notepad and pen as Gramps tinkered with something or the other and recounted adventures he'd had driving the car as a boy. She whirled toward Josh. "We can't let it be stolen!"

"I don't intend to."

His confident tone quelled her alarm. Embarrassed she'd let it get the better of her, she gave him a lopsided smile. "Would you show me how it works, too?"

"Be happy to. First, I'll need to figure out what's wrong with it. Your gramps and I never did get it running reliably again. I'll take a look at it this afternoon, after I get those cameras up. If I can get it working, we can take it out after church tomorrow, if you like."

Becki gave him an impulsive hug. "Thank you!"

Josh folded his arms around her. "My pleasure, Bec."

The tender sound of his pet name for her momentarily stayed her instinct to pull back. Since learning of her grandparents' deaths, she'd felt so alone. Josh was the only one to comfort her who really cared.

"Maybe you and I could work on it together, like your gramps did with me after my dad died."

Reluctantly, she eased her arms from around him, questioning the wisdom of jumping at reasons to spend *more* time with him. But one look at his red-rimmed eyes and she squeezed her own shut and laid her head against his chest. "You miss them as much as I do."

He rested his cheek against her hair. "Yes, I do."

Remembering the secret Anne had shared about how Josh blamed himself for her grandparents' deaths, Becki hugged him harder.

"Well, well, well," a familiar voice drawled from the direction of the door. "Settling right in, I see."

Becki sprang from Josh's arms. Smoothed her hair. "Neil? What are you doing here?"

"I thought you might need some help moving in." His muddy-blond hair was moussed back, his shirt and pants perfectly pressed, his polished shoes not the least bit appropriate for traipsing across the overgrown yard. His gaze drifted up Josh's full six feet and narrowed on his face. Neil pushed up his glasses with a single finger to the bridge. "But I see you're covered."

Was it her imagination or were the two of them puffing out their chests like rival birds fighting over a mate?

Yeah, right. She let out a choked snort. Definitely her imagination.

"How did you find me? I mean…" She hadn't given anyone from work her new address. The dusty barn air seemed to close in on her.

"Looked up the address on the internet. I remembered you mentioning your grandfather lived in Serenity." Neil stepped closer, arm outstretched toward Josh. "Neil Orner."

Josh gave Neil's hand a swift shake. "Joshua Rayne."

"Josh is my new neighbor and an old family friend," Becki rushed to explain. "He was just comforting me over my loss." She squirmed at how defensive that sounded. She didn't owe

Neil an explanation. They hadn't dated for over three months. "Um, Neil is a colleague from work," she said to Josh.

A muscle in Neil's cheek ticked, but what did he expect her to say?

Josh hooked his thumbs in the front pockets of his jeans. "I don't think Bec ever told me. Where is it you work?"

Neil inhaled, appearing to grow another half inch. "We work at Holton Industries."

Josh's jaw dropped a fraction, his eyes widening as he turned his attention back to her. "Industry?" He sounded skeptical. "I always figured you'd go into something to do with writing or graphic arts."

He thought about her?

"You never went anywhere without a pad and paper." A far-off look flickered in his eyes and a smile whispered across his lips as if he was picturing her as that tagalong girl again.

"That's fine for a hobby," Neil interjected. "But one can hardly make a living—"

"I don't know. If you're doing something you love, the rest seems to take care of itself."

Becki's chest swelled at Josh's defense, but his quiet confidence didn't seem to convince Neil. Of course, Josh had never needed much to be content, whereas Neil always wanted whatever seemed just out of reach. He'd admitted to being a bit of a runt growing up and seemed determined to put the ridicule behind him by latching onto the latest status symbols, which before they broke up had started to include an obsessive interest in her career decisions. That thought made her jittery all over again.

She closed the Cadillac's door, willing steel into her backbone. "Well, with any luck I'll find a job I love right here in Serenity."

Josh rested his hand at her waist, and his touch calmed her instantly. He urged her toward the barn door. "No luck needed. We'll pray you do."

The confidence in Josh's voice raised goose bumps on her arms. Stepping outside, she turned her face to the sun, wishing she could believe prayer would make a difference.

She once had. All those summers here, God had seemed so real. Even when He didn't answer her prayer that she be allowed to stay with Gran and Gramps after the divorce, she'd clung to Gran's assurances that God worked all things together for good. But how could any good come from letting Gran and Gramps die of carbon-monoxide poisoning?

Clearly, from the sour look on Neil's face, he didn't believe prayer would make a difference, either.

A cell phone rang, and both men reached for their hips.

"It's mine," Josh said. He glanced at the screen, then caught Becki's gaze. "Excuse me a sec." He stepped away from them, his phone to his ear.

"Why don't I give you a hand with those boxes in your car?" Neil suggested.

"I can't believe you came all the way out here."

He shrugged. "What's a three-hour drive to help a *friend?*"

She winced, certain his emphasis on *friend* was a dig to her "colleague" reference. "Last time we talked you told me I was crazy to want to move here."

"Still think so. Figured I'd come see what the attraction was." His gaze strayed to Josh, and he snorted. "I talked to Peters. He's going to fill your job with a temp for a few months. Give you a chance to decide if this is really what you want."

"I've already made my decision." She fisted her hands. This was the kind of I-know-what's-best-for-you attitude that had made her break up with him in the first place. He was more controlling than her mother.

"Don't be mad." He tucked an errant curl behind her ear. "You know you don't belong here."

She jerked away from his touch and stalked to her car.

"Rebecca." He trailed after her. "I was just trying to help. Country living may not be as great as you remember."

She opened the back door of her car, tugged out a box and plopped it into his arms. "I appreciate that. Really I do." She grabbed another box and led the way to the front door. "But you shouldn't have interfered."

"You're still mad at me because I didn't make it to your grandparents' funeral, aren't you?"

"What? No!" She shifted her box onto one hip and shoved her key into the door lock. "I never expected you to."

"I should have been there for you." He covered her hand and turned the key, pushing open the door.

She snatched her hand back and plowed past him into the house. She set the box on the old deacon's bench in the front hall, averse to inviting Neil any farther.

"Hey, no matter what else happens, we *are* friends. Right?"

She stared at him, a tad uneasy about what exactly that meant to him.

"Where do you want these?" Josh's voice drifted through the door, wrapping around her ragged nerves like a soothing hug. He held a stack of boxes in his arms.

She rushed forward and grabbed the one teetering from the top. "The living room is fine. Thanks."

"This, too?" Neil asked.

"No. It can stay here. Could you grab the boxes from the trunk next?"

The instant Neil went back outside, Josh stepped up behind her. "Do you mind if I do a quick walk-through? Make sure everything's okay?"

"Yes, thank you." Her words came out breathlessly. From the possibility that the prowler had been inside, she told herself, *not* from Josh's proximity.

Becki hurried out after Neil, before he got too curious. One time she'd caught him peeking in her desk drawers while he waited for her to finish getting ready for a date. He'd said he'd been looking for scissors to clip off a loose thread, and maybe he had been, but he had no sense of boundaries. Clearly.

If he did, he wouldn't be there.

It was one thing to stop by her desk and chat for a few minutes every day. It was entirely another to drive three hours to do it.

She'd appreciated that he had the self-confidence not to let their breakup ruin their working relationship. And okay, it had been really thoughtful of him to bring over supper and flowers from everyone at the office after she'd gotten word about her grandparents' deaths and left work so suddenly.

But now that their professional relationship had ended, she really didn't want to deal with him anymore.

"What does your neighbor do for a living?" Neil asked, passing her with an armload stacked even higher than Josh's had been.

She grabbed the top two boxes. "He's a police officer."

Neil gave a start. "That's handy."

"What do you mean?"

"If you have any trouble."

She pressed her lips closed, loath to admit she'd already had some. That was just the kind of thing Neil would latch onto to try to change her mind about moving here. He and her sister should start a club.

Josh met them at the door. He waited for Neil to pass by, then pulled her aside. "I need to go. They've found a submerged car in the old quarry and need a diver to check for… anything suspicious."

She gasped, certain he'd been about to say *bodies.* "I didn't realize you were a diver."

"Trained in the military." His eyes were shadowed. "Will you be okay?"

"Of course. Go."

"There's no sign your prowler got into the house, and I don't think he'll come around in daylight, especially with a couple of cars in the driveway. But if you see anything suspicious, don't hesitate to call me. Okay?" He pressed a business card into her hand with a number scrawled on the back. "That's my cell number."

For some reason Josh's protective concern didn't feel so condescendingly suffocating as Neil's always had. Maybe because the concern didn't seem so irrational coming from a cop. "I'll be fine."

"I'll be back as soon as I can." He lifted a hand to Neil, who'd stepped back into the foyer from wherever his curiosity had taken him while she'd been distracted by Josh. "Nice meeting you, Neil. See you around."

Neil sidled up to her as she watched Josh jog across the driveway back to his house. "He sounds worried about you. Not on my account, I hope."

She let out a puff of air—half cough, half snort. "Uh, no."

"Then why?"

"It was a little unsettling being back here for the first time with Gran and Gramps gone," she said evasively.

"I'd be happy to stick around for a while. Keep you company."

"Actually, I'd rather be alone right now." She tilted her head and added softly, "You understand?"

He clasped her upper arms and pressed a kiss to her forehead. "Of course. Let me just grab the housewarming gift I brought you."

She stood in the doorway, her arms wrapped around her waist, feeling like an ingrate, as he hurried to his flashy Mustang. He'd driven all this way to extend his help and friendship. The least she could do was offer him a cup of coffee before he left.

He opened his door and pulled out a hanging basket overflowing with fuchsia-colored dianthus. He strode toward her with a wide grin. "Do you like them?"

"They're beautiful. Thank you."

"I remembered you telling me how your gran used to have them hanging from the beams of the wraparound porch."

"You remembered that?" He'd never seemed to be listening.

"Of course." He patted the rails. "It's just like you described." He reached over her head and looped the basket onto a hook in the beam. "There."

"Would you like a glass of lemonade before you leave?" she blurted on impulse. Lemonade at least would be quicker than coffee. Gran always had a mix in the cupboard.

"That's okay. I know you have a lot to do. I just wanted to make sure you got here all right. And let you know that if you change your mind about staying..."

"I won't."

His eyes flicked around the yard, to the fields surrounding the two houses and to the thick stand of trees beyond. "It doesn't scare you to be out the back of nowhere? With next to no neighbors?"

"I won't change my mind," she said more adamantly.

He held his hands up in surrender. "Okay. I'm just saying if you did, no one would blame you. Not with who knows what kind of wild animals stalking those woods. Or creeps prowling for easy prey."

THREE

Josh shone his waterproof flashlight in, under and around the submerged car, fanned the search out another ten yards in every direction, then kicked to the surface. Hailing the officer in charge of the recovery, Josh pulled the regulator from his mouth. "It's clear."

"Good." Walt passed Josh the tow cable. "Hook her up. Then check the rest of the pit."

Josh reinserted his mouthpiece, then dived to the bottom with the cable and secured the towline to the car's frame. It'd take him another hour at least to thoroughly search every corner of the former quarry. Most of it was under eight feet or less of water, but one of the guys had said it got as deep as forty in the northeast corner. He kicked out of the way of the vehicle and surfaced long enough to signal it was okay to start towing.

He didn't want to spend any more time out here than he had to. He couldn't get that Neil guy off his mind. Bec hadn't seemed all that comfortable with him, and Neil clearly hadn't been deterred.

Josh didn't like how fidgety the guy had made her. Thanks to her prowler, she'd been jittery enough already. She didn't need an unwelcome wannabe boyfriend insinuating himself into the situation. And any guy who traveled this far just to check up on her had to have been more than a colleague, *or wanted to be*.

Josh clawed through the water, scoping every rock crevice. Had he been too quick to take Bec's word that she was okay being left alone with Neil?

He was taking way too much interest in Bec's affairs. A carp jutted from behind the rock ahead of Josh, stirring up a cloud of silt. He treaded in one spot, waiting for the water to clear. At least he'd had the decency to let a woman go without argument when she turned him down. Maybe he should have run a background check on Neil, made sure the guy wasn't some sort of stalker.

He hadn't missed Neil's *You know you don't belong here,* which sounded too much like the note that had been waiting for Bec in her mailbox when she'd arrived.

Josh dived back under, swimming faster than ever. Broken beer bottles littered the bottom of the pit. The area had been a popular hangout for teens for as long as he could remember. Surprising there wasn't more graffiti on the rocks than the occasional heart framing lovers' initials.

His thoughts slipped back to Bec, or more precisely the strange feeling that had come over him when she'd given him that impulsive hug. It reminded him of the time she'd thanked him for rescuing her from the tree she'd gotten herself stuck in as a kid. Only, when he'd folded his arms around her, it hadn't felt the same at all. He probably should be relieved Neil had shown up when he had.

If she knew how he'd failed her grandparents, she wouldn't want him anywhere near her. She was too vulnerable right now, between coping with her loss and starting over in a new town, a new job. Moving into the house. And now this prowler. Josh needed to focus on keeping her safe. Not on how wonderful it had felt to hold a woman in his arms.

He gave a hard kick and propelled himself into the deeper water. A woman in his arms… He knew better than to let his thoughts wander into that territory. He supposed helping his old high-school pal bring in his hay yesterday had started it.

His friend's wife and young son had brought a picnic lunch to the field for them, the boy squealing with delight when Josh's friend tickled his sides as the wife looked on with a contented expression.

It was the kind of life Josh had always longed for.

He sliced his arms through the water, relying more heavily on the narrow beam of his flashlight as he pushed deeper. The same as he'd learned to do with God. The Lord had blessed him with a country home, a good job and plenty of friends, and had even brought his sister back to Serenity.

Wishing for more only led to a whole well of hurt.

Neil, on the other hand, didn't seem to be getting that message.

The vibration of the winding tow cable rippled through the water.

Josh beefed up his strokes. The sooner he covered the search area, the sooner he could get home.

A shadow fell over the water ahead of him. Glancing up, he spotted a signal buoy. He kicked to the surface.

"Over here," Walt shouted from a new position onshore.

Josh pulled the regulator from his mouth. "What's up?"

"You wanted me to let you know if your cell phone rang."

His pulse jerked. *Bec?* "What's the caller ID?"

"Hunter Madison."

Josh's heart settled back into a steady rhythm. "Okay, let it go to voice mail. I'll call him when I'm finished." Hunter probably just wanted to check on where to put the cameras.

Josh dived back under and swept his light in widening arcs. The fish had gone into hiding. Hopefully, Bec's prowler wouldn't do the same. The last thing Bec needed was weeks of worrying if and when the intruder would show up again.

He winged a prayer skyward that God would help him catch the guy quickly.

The water was crystal clear, tinted a nice aquamarine, thanks to the limestone. Maybe he'd bring Bec here sometime with the dog. She might get a kick out of hunting for fossils in the rocks. It'd help take her mind off her troubles for a while. That and going out in her grandfather's old Cadillac.

Her eyes had lit up at the prospect, and he couldn't deny he was more than happy to fulfill that particular wish.

Overhead, the water grew choppy from the car breaking the surface.

Josh waited for the tow truck to haul the car out onto the flat rock overlooking the mini-lake and then did a final sweep of the area, his thoughts already back at the farm.

Finding nothing, he kicked to the surface and climbed out.

Walt handed him a towel. "There's nothing suspicious in the car. What do you make of it?"

Josh yanked off his regulator and mask and dragged his mind back to the investigation. "There's no body. Kids likely stole the car for a joyride, then ditched the evidence." More likely kids in this case than the incident in Bec's barn... unfortunately.

"Kids don't usually think to pull plates."

"True. Could've been used in a crime, then dumped." Josh scrubbed his hair dry with the towel. "Get any hits with the car's make and model?"

"Nope, not within Niagara anyway. No unrecovered Plymouths of any model reported stolen in the last two years."

"So not insurance fraud."

Walt shrugged. "Could be from another region."

"That car hasn't been down there more than a week." Josh walked around the car and then, stepping back, studied the distinctive rear taillights.

"You recognize something?" Walt asked.

"Yeah." Josh clenched the towel in his fist. "I think it's

the same car I saw pull out of a farmer's field near my place last night…around the same time my new neighbor was attacked by a prowler."

Becki headed to the car to grab the last of her boxes and froze. A stone's throw away, a black SUV idled in Josh's driveway. The dark-haired guy behind the wheel squinted at her, then turned off his engine.

Her breath caught. Was he the prowler?

She glanced around. Where was Tripod?

The SUV's door opened, and the guy's enormous boots hit the gravel with a thud. Boots that could dispense with Josh's three-legged dog in one swift kick.

The guy peeled off a jacket and slapped a ball cap on his head, exposing tattooed, steely arms. He looked as if he hadn't shaved in two days. Army-olive fatigues completed the impression of a mercenary looking for action. The guy reached behind his seat.

Josh's words blasted through her mind. *Some guys would just as soon shoot a witness as run away.*

Becki whirled on her heel and ran for the house.

"Hey, hold up there. Are you Bec?"

Bec? She stopped two yards from the door. Josh was the only one who called her that. This had to be the friend he'd called about borrowing the cameras. She turned slowly and backed up another couple of steps just to be safe. "Who wants to know?"

A friendly grin—not in the least bit mercenary—dented his cheeks. "I'm Hunter." He lifted his hand. A couple of drab-colored boxes dangled from his fingertips. "Josh asked me to hang these up for you."

"Thank you," she squeaked, then cleared her throat and added, "I appreciate that. Follow me, and I'll show—"

A sporty green car turned into her driveway.

"Oh." She looked from the car to the barn.

"You see to your visitor," Hunter said. "I can find my way." He tipped his hat and devoured the distance to the barn in powerful strides.

Able to breathe again, she reasoned that if Josh trusted the guy, she could, too. But the message wasn't getting to her pounding heart. She turned to the approaching car. The place was starting to feel like Grand Central Station. She didn't recognize the middle-aged man behind the wheel, but he looked a whole lot safer than Rambo.

He parked behind her car and lowered his window. "You Graw's granddaughter?"

"Yes. May I help you?"

The man stepped out of his car. Unlike Rambo, he was dressed conservatively, with his hair neatly cut, and clean-shaven. Empathy shone from his eyes when he extended his hand. "Name's Henry Smith. Remember we talked on the phone a few days back?"

"Oh, yes. You're the friend of my grandfather's." On the phone, he'd sounded closer to Gramps's age.

He cupped her hand between his. "I wanted to drop by to give my condolences. Your grandfather was a dear friend."

She tilted her head. "You said you knew him through the antique-car club, is that right?"

"That's right." He released her hand and reached into the car. "I thought you might like this." He handed her an eight-by-ten photo of Gran and Gramps posing by their Cadillac in their period costumes.

"Oh, wow!" She savored her grandparents' smiling faces. "Thank you so much. It's lovely."

"Took that on our last tour together. Thought you'd like it."

Becki traced the hat her gran wore. "I used to love snapping Gramps's suspenders and trying on Gran's big floppy hats."

"Yup, those are great costumes. There'd be a lot of folks in the club who'd be happy to buy them from you if you wanted to sell. Might be interested in some myself if you have time for me to look them over."

"Oh." She fluttered her hand toward the barn. "I think they stored those with the car in the trailer, which isn't here right now. But I'm not ready to part with anything just yet."

"Of course not."

They stood in uncomfortable silence for a moment.

Becki hitched her thumb toward the house. "Would you like to come in for a cup of coffee?"

"Oh, no." He motioned toward her open trunk. "I can see you're busy. I just wanted to see you got the photo."

She grabbed the last two boxes from her car and closed the lid. "C'mon, I could use the break and I'd love to hear more about your trips with my grandparents."

"Well if you put it that way… There's nothing we car enthusiasts like to do more than talk about our cars. Except tour them, of course."

She chuckled, recalling countless Saturday afternoons sitting on the back porch, listening to Gramps and his buddies talk about cars. "What kind of car do you drive on the tours, Mr. Smith?" she asked, leading the way to the back porch.

"Call me Henry, please. Sure is a beautiful place your grandparents had here."

"I think so. Of course, my ex-boyfriend thinks I'm nuts to want to live out here. He thinks the seclusion and wild animals are way scarier than street crimes."

"Sounds like someone who's never spent a day in the country."

"You've got that right."

Henry's gaze drifted over her shoulder. "Not that fella, then?"

She glanced back at Hunter, who blended into the tree in his camouflage. "Uh, no. He's just a…neighbor." She motioned Henry to one of the porch chairs. "Just give me a minute to get the coffee."

Henry followed her as far as the open patio door. "Your grandfather had some car trouble on his last tour. If he didn't get the chance to fix it, I could take a look if you like."

Becki grabbed the coffee sweetener from the cupboard. "That's okay. My neighbor already offered." She poured their coffees and rejoined Henry outside. "So tell me about your last tour with Gran and Gramps."

"First, tell me about your plans. What will you do with the old Cadillac?"

"Um, not sure yet." Becki shoved away the guilty feeling that the car was too valuable to be lumped with "contents" in the will. She couldn't bear the thought of parting with the "old gal," knowing how much she'd meant to Gramps.

Henry sipped his coffee and shared a couple of touring yarns.

"Can you tell me about any more of my grandparents' adventures?" Becki asked.

He glanced at his watch. "I'm afraid they'll have to wait for another time. I need to get on the road." He patted his breast pocket, pulled out a pen and jotted a number on a scrap of paper. "Here's my number if you run into any trouble with the car that your neighbor can't handle."

"Thank you." She stood next to the driveway until he'd driven away, then returned inside and leaned against the closed door. For the first time since she'd arrived, she really absorbed the sight of her beloved grandparents' home. She inhaled, basking in the distinctive fragrance that was her grandparents'.

But the air smelled a bit stale. From being closed up so long, probably. She meandered from room to room, flinging open windows. The scraped paint on the bottom of the too-low window in the main-floor bathroom reminded her of the time she'd locked the window on her sister, who used to sneak in and out through it. Boy, did she get in trouble that night.

The house phone rang.

Becki hesitated. She didn't really want to talk to anyone else, especially someone who might not have heard that Gran and Gramps were gone.

She swallowed. More likely it was a telemarketer. Or maybe Mom checking in to make sure she'd arrived safely. Becki let out a puff of air. Yeah, in her dreams.

For most of her life, Mom had dictated what Becki could and couldn't do, who she could date, what extracurricular activities she could join, what college she should attend, but the instant Becki had the *gall* to defy her and move into an apartment, Mom had stopped showing *any* interest in what she did. Which was just one more way to control her.

Drawing in a deep breath, Becki snatched up the phone. "Hello."

No answer.

She listened for a moment, expecting an automated voice to kick in with a spiel about how she'd won a cruise to a Caribbean island.

"Hello?"

The line clicked off.

How rude. If someone dialed the wrong number, they should at least have the decency to say something. Then again...

The caller might have expected Gran or Gramps to answer and been thrown off by her much younger voice. Next time she'd have to identify herself.

Putting the call out of her mind, she grabbed a box marked Bedroom and meandered upstairs, letting memories whisper through her thoughts.

The same frilly pink curtains adorned the window of the bedroom that she and Sarah had shared the summers they'd visited. Gran's music box still sat on the nightstand, too.

Becki turned the mechanism, and the strains of "My Favorite Things" filled the room. As the last notes died away,

Becki returned the music box to the nightstand and wiped the moisture from her eyes.

Thank goodness Josh wasn't there to see her sniffle over every knickknack. It was one thing to cry at a funeral. Everyone expected that. But almost a month had passed since her grandparents' deaths.

She glanced out the window. Across the yard, Hunter stood, scrutinizing the cameras he'd positioned. Josh wasn't taking any chances on missing her prowler the next time around.

If only he'd been as diligent investigating the cause of Gramps's headache.

She bit her lip, ashamed by the thought. Logically, she knew her grandparents' deaths weren't Josh's fault. She certainly didn't blame him. But…

Ever since Anne had told her about Gramps's headache, Becki couldn't stop thinking about how differently things could have turned out if only…

She shoved the pointless wish from her mind and unpacked the box she'd carried up. She set her jewelry box and hairbrush on the dresser next to the flip book of Bible promises that had been there for as long as she could remember. The visible page, yellowed and curled at the edges, read, "And we know that all things work together for good to them who love God…"

Becki tossed the book into the empty box and trudged downstairs. Passing the thermostat, she flicked it off.

If the weather hadn't been so humid the night her grandparents had died, Gran would have had the windows open instead of letting Gramps turn on the air conditioner. The carbon monoxide wouldn't have had a chance to build up and claim their lives. If God really cared, He would have worked things differently.

Josh's promise to pray for a new job whispered through

her thoughts. How could he be so confident God would answer that prayer when He hadn't protected Gran and Gramps?

The phone's ring fractured the silence. She drew in a deep breath, mentally prepared her greeting, then lifted the receiver. "Hello, Graw residence, their granddaughter Becki speaking."

Again silence greeted her.

"Hello, is anyone there?" She strained to hear any background noise. The faint whirr of traffic maybe. Was Josh calling from the quarry and unable to hear her? "Hello," she said more loudly.

The line clicked off.

She dialed star sixty-nine to find out who her caller was. The automated computer voice informed her the number was private.

Had the caller deliberately blocked his or her identity?

What if it was the prowler calling to see if anyone was home?

Now he knew who she was!

A knock sounded at the back door. She jumped, sending the phone toppling off the end table. She grabbed the phone and peered around the corner to try to catch a glimpse of who was there.

"Miss Graw? It's Hunter."

Her breath whooshed from her chest. *Of course. Idiot.* The phone call had scrambled her brain. She set down the phone and hurried to the back door. "Sorry, I was—" she waved toward the other room "—on the phone."

"No problem. I just wanted to let you know the cameras are up and I'm heading out. You can hang on to them as long as you need them."

"Will do. Thank you so much. Can I get you a coffee or something before you go?"

He tipped his cap, his mouth spreading into an amused grin.

"That's okay. Maybe some other time when Josh is around." He winked, then strode across the yard back to his SUV.

Great, now he'd think his friend's new neighbor was a nervous Nellie. Of course, if he was in the habit of always dressing like Rambo, he probably got that reaction a lot. She flipped the dead bolt and returned to her unpacking.

A door upstairs slammed shut, making her jump yet again. *It's just the wind, you ninny.* She should probably shut the windows now that she was alone again.

She made quick work of the downstairs ones, then grabbed another box marked Bedroom and climbed the stairs. She wrestled the end room's window closed first. It opened to a meadow with a stand of trees beyond. Movement in the trees caught her attention. She squinted, hoping to spot a deer and her fawn. She'd have to find Gran's binoculars.

The phone rang as she reached her grandparents' bedroom. She snatched up their bedside extension, an old-fashioned rotary dial. "Hello."

Once again, an ominous silence greeted her.

"If you don't want to talk to me, stop calling." She slammed the phone down with a satisfying thwack. If the creep called one more time, she'd have him blocked. There had to be a way for the phone company to do that, even if he was hiding his number. She shut the back windows and was about to move to the front bedrooms when the phone rang again.

If she had a whistle, she'd be tempted to let it blast. She smiled to herself, then puckered up and put her thumb and forefinger between her lips as she lifted the receiver. She didn't say a thing and when the person on the other end didn't either, she let loose for a full ten seconds.

After a second's pause, a voice came on the line. "Bec? Is that you?"

"Josh? Uh, sorry about that. Someone's been calling here and not saying anything and then hanging up. I figured I'd give him an earful."

"When? How many times?"

His staccato questions set her pulse racing all over again. "Three times in the last half hour or so. I tried star sixty-nine, but the guy blocked his information."

"I'm on my way now. That's why I called. If the phone rings again, don't answer it. When I get there, I'll get hold of the phone company and have them trace the call."

Outside, Tripod started barking.

Sure, where was the dog an hour ago when Rambo showed up? "Your dog's going nuts over something outside."

"Probably a cat again. Can you see him?"

Becki unwound the phone cord from behind the night table and moved to the window to try and see what had him riled. A noise sounded from downstairs. The dog?

She couldn't see him from the window. From his barking, it sounded as if he was prancing back and forth along the west wall. She moved toward the bedroom door, straining to hear if the sound had really come from inside.

Another thump sounded.

"Josh," she whispered, "I think someone's in the house."

"Where are you?"

"Upstairs."

A voice spoke in the background, and then Josh barked orders to send a cruiser to her address. "Help is on the way, Bec. I'm fifteen minutes out." Through the phone, a siren whirred to life, while at her end, silence reigned.

The dog's not barking. She clenched the phone to her ear. "Josh, the dog's not barking!"

"It's going to be okay. I want you to hide in the bathroom. Lock the door."

"But I'm on an old plug-in phone, I'd have to hang up."

"Listen to me. You need to hang up. If the intruder sees a light on the downstairs phone, he'll know someone's in the house."

Her fingers tightened around the receiver at the thought of breaking the connection.

A loud pop and whoosh cracked the silence.

She gasped.

"What is it? What's going on?" The urgency in Josh's voice sent her pulse careening.

"A… It sounded like a gunshot. Outside."

"Are you sure it wasn't one of the bangers that scare birds from the vineyards across the road?"

Her heart pummeled her ribs as she tugged the phone as far as it would reach and tried to see out the front windows from the hallway. "I don't know. Maybe."

A second shot sounded. And a puff of dirt kicked up in the yard.

She dropped to her belly. "No, it's real. Someone's shooting at the house!"

FOUR

At the sound of dead air swallowing Bec's whispered "Hurry," Josh floored the gas pedal. What kind of car thief shot at a house?

Josh tightened his grip on the steering wheel. Was he reading the situation all wrong? Were the note, the incident in the barn and these shots really about scaring Bec off her grandparents' property?

He banked the corner too fast. His wheels bit into the graveled shoulder. He cranked the wheel hard to the left, then right, pulling the car straight, wishing he could get a grip as easily on what was going on.

The guy Bec had surprised in the barn had to believe she could identify him, or else why expose his proximity by shooting at the house?

Seven minutes out, his police radio blared to life. "We're on-site. No sign of an intruder outside. But no one's answering the door."

Josh snatched up the radio. "I told her to hide in the upstairs bathroom. Use the bullhorn."

Twenty long seconds later, an officer came back on. "Okay, we see movement... The front door's opening... A lone woman, Caucasian, curly hair."

Relief washed through him. "Yeah, that's her. Rebecca Graw," he confirmed.

"She's fine," the officer assured him.

A second voice cut in. "Need first aid. West side of the house. Hurry."

"Hunter?" Josh careened onto his road, a whole other fear welling inside him. "What you got?"

"It's Tripod." The harsh rattle in his friend's voice clutched at his throat. "He's been hit."

Josh screeched to a stop behind the row of police cars and raced to the side of the house. The circle of uniformed officers opened, and the officer in charge ordered a search for the shooter.

Bec was kneeling in front of a whimpering Tripod. She stroked the pup's head. "What a brave boy you are. A real guard dog."

Josh stared at them, his heart pummeling his chest.

Hunter, dressed in street clothes—he must have picked up the call on his police scanner—glanced up from examining the dog's lone back leg. "He'll be okay. Just a graze. The force must have knocked his foot out from under him."

Josh let out a breath and nodded. Hunkering beside Bec, he squeezed her shoulder and ruffled Tripod's ears with his other hand. "You did good, bud. Real good."

He cleared the emotions clogging his throat and rubbed slow circles on Bec's back. "You okay?" he whispered close to her ear.

She shook her head, moisture clinging to her eyelashes. "Why would someone do this?"

"I don't know. But I promise you we'll find him."

Hunter swabbed the dog's wound with antiseptic. "He should be as good as new in a day or two."

When Josh nodded his thanks, Hunter held his gaze. "We need Miss Graw to answer some questions." The unspoken question in his eyes asked if Josh could handle the job without becoming emotionally involved.

The answer was no, and Hunter clearly recognized as

much. This was little Becki Graw, the girl he'd been getting out of scrapes since she was knee-high. Of course this was personal. "I'll take care of it," Josh said. "Can you run a trace on incoming calls over the past hour?"

With a brisk nod, Hunter disappeared around the house.

Josh gently scooped Tripod into his arms. "We'll talk inside."

As they approached the front door, Hunter came out. A squirming cat leaped from his arms. Tripod tried to jump after it, but Josh held him fast.

"How'd that get inside?" Bec asked.

"Not sure. Found it cowering in the basement when I came in. Probably squeezed under the root-cellar door to get away from the dog. Knocked a canning jar off one of your shelves by the looks of it."

"That must be what you heard in the basement," Josh said to Bec before turning his attention back to Hunter. "See if the cameras picked up anything useful, will you?"

Bec led the way inside and spread a thick blanket on the carpet for Tripod. "Maybe the shots were from a hunter. Someone might have mistaken Tripod's movements in the woods for game."

"You said the shots were directed toward the house."

She smoothed the edges of the blanket. "I was rattled from the phone calls and Tripod's barking. Maybe I was wrong. Maybe he got winged by a hunter in the woods and then ran to the house."

"On the phone, you said you heard the dog barking at the house before the shot."

"Do you think a hunter could have misjudged the distance his bullet would travel?" Bec asked, clearly grasping for any explanation that would put some much-needed distance between her and this latest incident. Her fingers worried the edge of the blanket.

Josh covered her hands with his to still them. "It's not hunting season."

"How about a farmer? Aren't they allowed to take down an animal that goes after their stock?"

"Sure, but they wouldn't be doing that on your property." He decided against mentioning his suspicions about the abandoned car they'd found at the quarry. She was upset enough.

By the time Josh had gleaned every detail she could remember from the afternoon, Hunter had reappeared at the door. "The cameras didn't pick up anything, but we got a couple of numbers for those phone calls. Last one was yours. The other three came from a cell phone, but the number couldn't be traced."

"A pay-as-you-go?" Criminals' phone of choice.

"Yeah."

Josh rubbed his chin. "Could they tell how long ago the phone was activated?"

"Yesterday."

Bec's face blanched.

Josh motioned for Hunter to give them some privacy. After the door closed behind his friend, Josh touched his finger under Bec's chin and tipped her face toward him. "Tell me what you're thinking."

"Someone's going to a lot of trouble to scare me off this property."

Josh searched her eyes. "Do you still think it's your sister? That she hired someone to do this?"

"It's the only thing that makes sense, but I just can't believe she'd go this far. I mean…those were real bullets!"

Josh rubbed his palms up and down her upper arms. "Tell me about Neil."

She croaked out a laugh. "It couldn't be him."

"From where I was standing, he looked like exactly the kind of guy who'd stoop to scare tactics to get what he wanted."

"We're not even dating."

Josh dropped his hands to his sides. "Looked to me like that wasn't his choice."

Her face flushed a bright red. "He accepted my decision."

"On the surface maybe. But deep down, I'm thinking he figured you'd eventually come to your senses. Only, now you've moved outside his sphere of influence, so to speak."

She shook her head vehemently. "He doesn't own a gun. At least…I can't imagine him owning one."

"They're easy enough to come by." Josh's hand skimmed his own holstered weapon as he tried to tamp down his irritation that she was defending the guy.

Her chin dropped to her chest. She reached out a trembling hand and ruffled Tripod's fur. "I can't believe he'd… He wouldn't shoot a dog."

So she conceded that he might shoot off a gun to scare her into fleeing back to the city?

Josh pressed his lips together to stop himself from saying it. He definitely needed to do a background check on the creep.

The more he thought about it, a guy like Neil was exactly the type who'd take an interest in a collector's item like the 1913 Cadillac parked in the barn, too. He'd probably snuck into town ahead of Bec and planted that note in the mailbox, then got caught nosing around the barn and panicked.

"I was thinking…" Bec pushed the hair from her face and stiffened her spine. "Whoever made those calls must have been phoning to see if the place was empty so they could come back and steal the car."

"If he'd called once, maybe. But three times so close together? Not likely."

Her gaze drifted to an old family picture on the mantel of Bec and her sister. The muscles in her jaw flexed. Then suddenly she snatched up the phone.

"Who are you calling?"

"Sarah."

"I'm not sure that's such a—"

Wes, the officer directing the search, poked his head around the door. "Josh, can I have a word with you outside?"

"Be right back," he said to Bec. He joined the other officer on the porch. "What'd you find?"

"Two possibilities. Seems your dog's been ripping through the neighbors' farmyards chasing cats. One of your neighbors said it wouldn't be the first time a farmer's taken a pot-shot at a roving dog."

"He say which farmer?"

"Nope, but we found these in the dirt around the house." Wes held out his palm.

Josh examined the small hunks of metal. "Air-rifle pellets."

"Yup. Looks like our shooter was a kid playing around or someone who just wanted to scare the pup off."

"Or Becki."

Wes clapped his hand closed around the pellets. "My advice is that you keep your dog tied up and you won't have any more trouble."

Josh squared his jaw. "You said there were two possibilities?"

"Yeah." Wes glanced toward the barn. "Hunter said Miss Graw had an intruder last night messing with her grandfather's antique car."

"That's right."

"A few weeks back we got a call from a police officer in the Ottawa area, asking questions about Graw and his car."

"What kind of questions?"

Wes hesitated, his reluctance to say etched in his face.

"What kind of questions?" Josh repeated.

"Like if Graw was the kind of man who could pull off a jewelry heist."

"A jewelry heist?" Josh almost laughed at the absurdity of the idea.

"Seems they had some expensive pieces lifted from a museum that the antique-car club toured. A tour Graw was on. A tour he'd left two days early."

Josh shook his head. "You know Graw would never have been mixed up in anything like that."

"I know."

"So what did you tell the officer?"

"That Graw was dead."

"Are you nuts?" her sister screamed. "What kind of person do you think I am?"

Becki jerked the phone away from her ear. "The kind who'd go to any lengths to ensure I sell this house so that you get a bigger piece of the pie."

Sarah gasped. "I'd never threaten you. Never."

"You threatened to go to the lawyer if I didn't cave…and then did!"

Josh walked in the door, his expression grim.

"The police officer's back. I've got to go. But make no mistake, if they find proof it was you, I don't care if you are my sister, I will press charges." Becki disconnected before Sarah could respond.

Josh's mouth twisted to one side. "I take it she denied any involvement."

"Yup."

"Do you believe her?"

Becki hesitated. "I don't know. Her horrified gasp sounded real enough." Becki turned the phone over in her hands. "And she was home, so clearly she didn't pull the trigger. But maybe she just couldn't believe what her hired henchman would do. What did that officer have to say?"

Josh glanced away, and Becki recognized the tic in his cheek. He'd had the same reaction the time her favorite kitten had been hit by the hay wagon and he didn't want to tell her. He'd always gone above and beyond to try to protect her, even as a teenager. Given how insensitive her parents had been, Becki had always appreciated Josh's acute regard for her feelings.

"I'm a big girl now," she reminded him, setting the phone back on the table.

He took a seat. "It's good news, in a way." Leaning forward, he clasped his hands between his knees. "The shots came from an air rifle, which means they weren't intended to do more than frighten."

"Me or the dog?"

"I'm not sure." The concern in his gaze made her heart stutter. "Wes thinks the dog. One of the neighbors said as much."

"But you still think it's Neil?"

That muscle in his cheek twitched again. "I just don't like coincidences. Those phone calls are suspicious. I still want to check into his whereabouts. How soon did he leave here this morning?"

"Not long after you left."

Becki snatched up the phone again.

"Who are you calling?"

"Neil's house number. If he's home already, then there's no way he could be the one who fired those shots."

Neil picked up on the second ring.

Becki let out a breath of relief that her former relationship hadn't morphed into a *Fatal Attraction* remake. She quickly fabricated a story about feeling bad that she'd sent him off so quickly after he'd traveled so far to visit her, then thanked him again for the flowers.

"My pleasure, Rebecca. I'll try to make it down there again soon, and you can show me the sights."

Becki cringed at how he'd instantly mistaken her apology for interest. "Uh, there's not much to do but watch the grass grow here, remember? Not your idea of a good time."

"Any time with you is good."

She swallowed a gag, which wasn't fair. He sounded sincere…unfortunately. Becki threw Josh a desperate look, but he was absorbed in a conversation on his cell phone. "Uh, sorry, Neil, I've got to run. My neighbor just came to the door."

Neil's snort and terse goodbye left no doubt as to his opinion of Josh.

Good. Maybe that would stave off any more surprise visits.

"You're certain?" Josh clutched his phone with white-knuckled fingers, piquing Becki's curiosity. He glanced her way and quickly ended the call.

"Who was that?" she asked.

"It's not important."

"It sounded important."

He tucked his phone into his pocket. "Nothing for you to worry about. So what did Neil say?"

"Since he was home, I didn't want to mention what happened. Would only fuel his arguments against my moving here."

Josh nodded, but he looked as if he wanted to say more.

"Maybe that officer is right about the shots." Catching herself nervously twisting her necklace, she pressed her palms to her thighs. "I was so worked up with everything that happened yesterday and then the phone calls that I freaked. Obviously a car thief isn't going to start shooting at the house and draw attention to himself. He'd just wait until I'm out."

Josh squeezed her hand. "It's always better to call for help than regret it later. And don't forget one of those pellets winged Tripod."

The dog whimpered at his name.

Becki slipped her hand free from Josh's reassuring grasp and stood. She couldn't let herself start leaning on him. "I'd better finish unpacking."

Josh scraped his hand over his jaw. "How about I leave Tripod here with you tonight?"

She tilted her head and squinted at him, but she couldn't read his expression. "What aren't you telling me?"

"Bec, I don't want you to worry unnecessarily."

"O-kay…"

"Does Neil have call forwarding?"

"I don't know." A lump balled in her throat. "Why?"

"Because he's not answering his door."

You don't belong here.

Becki surged from her bed and paced the bedroom floor for the umpteenth time.

Tripod whined at being disturbed yet again. Josh had left him with her—for company, he'd said, but more likely so the dog would bark if anyone tried to break in.

Becki scratched his ears. "I'm sorry, boy, but your master has my stomach in knots. First he convinces me it's got to be Neil who's terrorizing me. Then he tells me not to worry even though Neil never showed up at his apartment tonight."

She inched aside the curtains and peered at the yard bathed in moonlight. Leafy shadows danced on the barn wall. *It doesn't scare you to be out the back of nowhere? With next to no neighbors? And who knows what kind of wild animals stalking those woods?*

She took a deep breath and slowly released it. Neil had just been trying to manipulate her. No one was out there.

She wasn't going to let Neil, or her sister, coerce her into leaving. First thing Monday morning, she'd call her old boss and tell him not to bother holding her job as Neil had suggested, and then she'd call Gramps's lawyer to find out if Sarah had any chance of challenging the will. Relieved to have a plan of action, she crawled back into bed and mashed her pillow into a new shape.

Something creaked.

Her eyes flew open. The wispy white sheers fluttered at the

window, looking ghostlike with the moonlight shimmering through them. Becki slanted a peek at Tripod. Still sleeping.

She reined in her galloping heart. If the noise had been an intruder, the dog would have been alerted. Surely.

The creak sounded again.

Only, it was more of a whistle. The wind sneaking through the eaves?

Fixing her gaze on the fluttering curtains, she listened more closely. How had she not noticed the peepers chirruping like a rock concert gone wild outside, punctuated by the bullfrog's occasional *owooga?*

She huffed onto her side and tried to ignore them. Then just as she'd gotten used to the "music," the critters invited a new voice to the party—the thrumming bass strings of some other amphibian.

"Aaaah!"

Tripod instantly lifted his head and gave her a worried look.

"Sorry, boy. Go back to sleep." One of them might as well. She snapped on the bedside lamp and shimmied up to lean against the headboard.

The phone rang.

She tensed. This couldn't be happening. Not again. Not at—she peered at the clock—three in the morning. What had Josh told her to do?

She scrubbed her head, trying to clear her foggy brain.

The phone blasted again.

She snatched it up.

"Bec, you okay?" Josh's sleep-roughened voice wrapped around her heart and slowed it to an even gallop. "I saw your light come on."

She glanced back to the window. Through the sparse line of trees that separated her house from Josh's, she could just make out a light.

He sounded as if he'd just awakened, and the thought that

he'd been watching her place so diligently that he'd noticed her light come on in the wee hours of the morning chased the chill that had gripped her.

"Bec?" he repeated, concern pitching the question up an octave.

She tried not to read more into his concern than there was. He was, after all, a police officer. Protecting people from intruders was his job. "I couldn't sleep for the frog noises. Do you have any idea how many different sounds they make?"

He chuckled. "And knowing your imagination, you sectioned them into orchestra parts."

"A rock band, actually," she admitted, heartened that he remembered their evenings sitting around the campfire with Gran and Gramps, making up stories about the night sounds.

Josh's laugh eased the last of her tension. "Tripod okay?"

"Sleeping like a baby. I'm sorry I woke you."

His snort suggested that he hadn't been able to sleep, either, despite the gravelly sound of his voice. She really should let him try. No reason both of them should be tossing all night.

"Have you tried counting sheep?" he asked.

"Just wolves."

He groaned. "We're going to catch this guy. I promise you." His earnestness wound around her heart the way his strong arms had protectively wrapped around her earlier. Oh, boy, she should so not be going there.

As noble as Josh was, sentry duty was bound to get old quick. "Um, I think I'll just read for a bit. Get my mind off… things."

"You sure?"

"Yes." Who was she kidding? She'd just traded one preoccupation for another. But thankfully, Josh took her at her word and said good-night. The last thing she wanted was for him to feel as if he had to constantly watch out for her like a big brother. She slipped the phone back onto the nightstand. "Or worse, like some rescued stray."

Tripod lifted his head and whimpered.

"No offense, bud. Josh loves you. I'm sure he'll never get tired of having you around." Not the way her dad had forced them to give up their one and only dog after less than three weeks.

Not wanting to remember other things Dad had quickly tired of—including her—Becki pulled one of Gran's photo albums onto her lap. Mom and Dad had never taken pictures of them, so Becki and her sister had relished posing for the camera whenever they visited Gran and Gramps.

Gran had written little notes beneath each one, too.

Becki traced her finger over a picture of Gramps carrying her on his shoulders in front of the house. She couldn't have been more than five or six. Beneath the picture Gran had written, "Our Becki says she wants to live here always, even when she's big."

Not like her daddy.

Gran would never have written the words that whispered through Becki's thoughts, but she knew that Dad's restlessness had always tugged at Gran's heart. Becki had never understood why her dad had loathed Serenity so much. He was the polar opposite of Josh.

She forced her mind away from Josh and back to her dad. He'd rarely stuck around for more than a day when they visited Gran and Gramps, leaving them time alone with Mom.

Before long, Gran had invited her and Sarah to visit without their parents, which had suited Becki just fine. Poor Gran must have grieved all over again when Mom moved halfway across the country and stopped sending them, too, with her default "it's for the best" excuse.

Becki traced Gramps's smiling face. *Becki wants to live here always.* Is that why they'd left her the place?

She'd loved everything about her grandparents' home, from sliding down the banister to swinging on the big oak tree out back. She'd loved that Gran never lamented how impossible it was to pull the comb through Becki's tangle of curls. She'd loved that Gramps never complained how many dishes she'd broken with her butterfingers.

When she would return from playing in the woods, covered from head to toe in mud, they would chuckle instead of scold. And she hadn't minded at all that Gran hosed her down outside with the icy well water before allowing her to step foot in the bathroom.

Becki smiled at the memory of Josh getting a blast of that same water a time or two.

Stop thinking about him already! She slammed the photo album shut and clicked off the light.

Somewhere between the frogs winding down their concert and her snuggling deeper under the comforter, thoughts of Josh must have turned to dreams, because the next thing she knew, a *ping* on the window jolted her awake.

She blinked at the bright sunlight beaming through the sheers.

"Hey, sleepyhead. You still in bed?" Josh's amused voice filtered through her fuzzy brain.

Terrific. He wasn't helping. How was she supposed to keep her mind off him if he showed up at her window, jolting her awake as if fifteen years had evaporated overnight and they'd sneak in an early-morning fishing trip before church?

Then again, maybe they could just skip church. She pulled on her bathrobe. He'd simply taken for granted that she'd attend. She swept aside the curtains. "Don't you know it's bad manners to—" The rest of Becki's thought flew from her head at the sight of Josh looking up at her second-story window wearing a handsome blazer, a crisply pressed shirt and tie, and a grin that turned her inside out.

FIVE

Josh whistled as he waited for Bec to come downstairs with Tripod. He'd hated to wake her so early after the night she'd had, but if the dog didn't get outside soon, she'd hate him more.

Tossing pebbles at her bedroom window had felt like old times. Good times. Times when summers were carefree and the worst they could imagine happening was falling from a tree.

The instant her kitchen door opened and Tripod dashed out, Josh stepped up with the tray of coffee and bagels he'd brought with him. "Not as fancy as my sister's breakfast, but after the trouble you had sleeping, I figured you could use a jolt of caf—"

The sight of her soft, sleep-rumpled face swept the words clean out of his head.

She pushed the door wider and motioned him inside. "Thanks."

Struggling to ignore what the crackly, early-morning texture of her voice did to him, he carried the tray into the kitchen and helped himself to a mug of coffee. "Uh…" He hadn't been able to really see her up at the bedroom window, and now that he could…

He finished his coffee in three burning gulps and set it back on the tray. "I'd better wait for you outside."

Her brow creased. Then she swiped at the lines crisscrossing her cheeks from where she'd slept and scrunched together the neck flaps of her white terry robe.

He dropped his gaze to the floor, feeling bad that he'd made her self-conscious.

Her bare toes, with their hot-pink polish, wiggled.

The fact she painted her usually hidden toenails and yet didn't seem to wear makeup sparked even more curiosity about this utterly grown-up version of the cute kid he used to rescue from the old oak tree.

She cleared her throat, jerking his attention back to her face.

His own flamed. Okay, this was definitely *not* a good idea. "Uh…" He hitched his finger over his shoulder. "I need to feed the dog. Come get me when you're ready to leave for church. Okay?"

"Actually…" She stirred her coffee, her unsweetened, black coffee that didn't need stirring. "I was thinking maybe I'd skip church today. I'm not really up to facing—"

"We can take the Cadillac," he blurted on impulse. Anything to convince her not to stay home alone. He'd just have to call Hunter and alter their plan a bit.

Her eyes lit up. "You got it going?"

"Yup. Turns out it was just a bad connection. Finally found the problem this morning." He wasn't sure what had compelled him to work on the car again this morning. In the back of his mind, he must've known he'd need the carrot. He hadn't told her what Wes had said about the jewelry theft.

Not that he believed for a second that Bec's grandfather had anything to do with the robbery.

But the person who'd been poking around the place might. Might even have been poking around before Bec had arrived. Maybe even had tampered with the hot-water tank.

His stomach knotted. No, the service tech had insisted

the squirrel nest blocking the chimney was to blame for the carbon monoxide.

"So…" he said, hoping his teasing tone didn't sound as forced to her ears as it did to his own. "Want to change your mind?"

She bobbed her head from side to side. "We could just go cruising after church like we'd planned."

"We could…. But do you really want me to worry about you being here alone all morning? I might get too stressed to drive this afternoon."

She rolled her eyes. "You're determined to guilt me into this, aren't you? Or scare me."

"Whatever works." He gave her a wicked grin.

"Okay, okay. I'll go. Just give me an hour to shower and dress. And wake up!"

"Perfect. That'll give me enough time to pull the old gal out and dust her off." And contact Hunter to put a new plan in place. Maybe Wes could stake out the church parking lot once they parked the Caddy, and Hunter could still keep an eye on the house, in case Bec's prowler decided to take advantage of the time she'd be tied up in church.

With fifteen minutes to spare, Bec showed up on his doorstep dressed to turn every bachelor's head within a hundred miles. Wow. The instant he stepped through the church doors with Bec in that frothy vanilla sundress with her hair tamed by the doodad accessories that let the most becoming tendrils slip free to frame her face, he'd be the envy of every guy in the place.

She tugged at a wisp of hair, which sprang back to its curly Q shape the instant she released it. "That bad? It's impossible to do anything with it in the humidity."

"It looks fine," he said.

She frowned, and he winced at how gruff he'd sounded. It wasn't her fault he'd suddenly noticed how attractive she was.

Oh, boy. Maybe this wasn't such a good idea. Not to mention how carpooling together to church and then sharing a pew was bound to wind up the rumor mill, especially when the favorite pastime of the church's older ladies seemed to be trying to hook him up with a woman. As if he needed any more reminders of how big a failure he was at romance.

He gritted his teeth and reminded himself they meant well. How were they to know that every woman he'd ever dated chose something better over him?

Bec flounced past him toward the car. Her exotic scent caught him by surprise. As a kid she'd always smelled like sunshine and flowers, except for the time…

He bit back a grin. "You sure smell better than the time you fell into that stagnant pond."

She stuck out her tongue. "Thanks for reminding me."

"No problem. What are friends for?"

"Neil actually gave me this perfume."

The grin slipped off Josh's face.

Bec waved her wrist in front of his nose. "Do you like it?"

No. "To tell you the truth," he hedged, "I always pictured you more of a sunshine-and-roses kind of girl."

She drew back her arm. "Well, in case you hadn't noticed, I'm not a girl anymore."

"Yeah, kind of noticed," he muttered under his breath and stopped alongside the car. "So Miss Grown-Up, does that mean you do or don't want the car's top down?"

"Oh, I almost forgot!" She rummaged through her purse and drew out a cowboy-style kerchief, which she draped over her head and tied under her chin. In an instant she went from runway worthy to schoolgirl.

Josh couldn't help it. He laughed.

"Oh, if you think this looks funny, you'd bust a gut over what the wind would do to my hair if I didn't wear it."

"I'll leave the top up."

"Doesn't help much when the car has no side windows!"

"Good point." He opened the passenger door, and Bec climbed in. He quirked an eyebrow. "You driving?"

She squinted up at him. "Not until you teach me how this thing works."

"Well, then…" He motioned to the driver's side—the right side of this particular car—where the would-be door was blocked by the stick shift and brake lever. "You going to let me in?"

"Oops." She scurried out. "I forgot."

He slid across the seat, and she climbed back in. "Okay. First lesson." He quickly showed her the positions of the gearshift, then moved it into Neutral and pushed the red ignition button on the dash.

The engine sputtered to life.

"That's it?" she asked.

"When all goes as it should, yes."

"And when it doesn't?"

He gunned the gas. "It's a lot more complicated than we have time for right now."

They settled into a rambling forty miles per hour, and Bec inhaled deeply. "I've missed the smell of country air."

"Cow manure?"

She swatted his arm. "I'm serious. As soon as the smell of hay and clean air and, yes, animals wafted through my car windows yesterday, I knew I'd found my way home."

The wistful way she said *home* made his heart skip a beat, but he couldn't help but wonder if her feelings would last. Lots of people fell in love with country living in the long, lazy days of summer, but their attitudes changed come February when winter entrenched itself in the community and showed no sign of releasing its grip for another two months.

"But I'm preaching to the choir. Right?"

"Yup," he confirmed and reminded himself that she was a city woman now. Not the girl who'd begged not to have to leave at the end of every summer and who'd always been humming one Sunday-school chorus or another.

She chattered on about various day trips she and her grandparents had taken in the car, but the closer they got to the church, the quieter she grew.

"You okay?" he asked finally.

"I'm not sure I can do this."

"It's okay to cry, Bec. I know I did at more than one service after my dad died."

"You did?" She suddenly sounded so lost.

"Yes," he said gently. He shifted the gear stick into First, so a kid couldn't accidentally start the car rolling, then pulled up the brake lever. "Trust me. Everyone understands." He reached across the seat and squeezed her hand. "You'll be okay."

She dragged the scarf from her head, took a deep breath and released it slowly. "Okay, I'm ready."

As he waited for her to climb out ahead of him, he nodded to Wes, who'd positioned his truck near the exit where he could easily intercept a possible car thief.

When Josh looked back at Bec, Bill Netherby, a local farmer who had a knack for instantly turning strangers into friends, was pumping her hand.

"Becki, welcome back. We were so glad to hear that your grandparents' place is staying in the family, and—" he gestured toward the Cadillac "—I'm glad to see you didn't take that fella up on his offer to buy the old car."

Josh clambered out of the front seat to join Bec. "What fella?"

Bill looked from Josh to Bec's equally curious expression. "Didn't he find you? The night before last, I was out on my bicycle down your way, and this fella asked directions to your place. Said he saw your grandparents' death notice in the car-club magazine, alongside a picture of the car. I figured he wanted to make an offer."

Bec's gaze darted to Josh.

He nodded, silently acknowledging her suspicion that the guy might have been her attacker. "You catch the guy's name?" he asked Bill.

"Afraid not, sorry."

"Could you describe him?"

"Not much to describe. Average height, average build. Dark hair. Middle-aged. Can't think of anything about him that really stood out."

"A beard? A mustache? An accent, maybe?"

"Like I said, he was pretty average."

"What kind of car did he drive?"

"An old green Plymouth."

Josh's pulse spiked. The same color and make they'd pulled out of the quarry. Had the guy known Josh spotted the car and decided to dump it? "Thanks, Bill. We'll be sure to keep an eye out for him." Josh prodded Bec forward.

She dug in her heels and whirled on him. "What are we going to do?"

"Like I said, keep an eye out for him." Josh pulled out his cell phone and texted the new information to the officer investigating the abandoned car, then sent the suspect's description—for what it was worth—to Wes and Hunter.

"This helps, right?" Bec's voice hummed with nervous energy. "I mean, this has got to be the same guy who knocked me out and then made those phone calls and shot at the house. And it can't be Neil. No one would ever peg him as average."

Josh pictured the man's horn-rimmed glasses and pointy nose. "No, probably not." His background check on her ex hadn't turned up so much as a parking ticket, either, and no Plymouths registered to him. For the first time since failing to locate Neil after yesterday's visit, Josh could take a full breath. He'd rather deal with a thwarted car thief than an ex.

He turned to escort Bec inside, but the sight of Bart Winslow watching her with a predatory gleam from the front seat of his Maserati pitched his good mood into a tailspin.

If not for Netherby's encounter with the stranger interested in the Cadillac, Josh could imagine, only too well, Bart being behind the attacks on Bec.

The thirty-year-old son of the town's slimiest real-estate agent was the kind of jerk who would stoop to any tactics to help out his dad. And his dad's current pet interest was snatching up rural properties for development.

Properties like Bec's.

The rigid line of Josh's jaw sent Becki's pulse spiking. She tracked his gaze to a red car parked on the street. A casually dressed blond-haired guy sat inside. "Who's that?" she asked.

Anne swooped up from behind them and hooked her arm through Josh's. "The best-looking and most eligible bachelor in town."

Josh gave his sister a withering look. "If you prefer the partying, fast-driving type. C'mon, let's go inside and find a seat." He grazed his fingertips across Becki's back.

She started, caught off guard by the jitters his touch unleashed, and scrambled to gather her wits. She'd been so preoccupied with worrying about breaking down into a blubbering fool the moment she stepped inside the church that she hadn't been paying attention to her inconvenient reactions to Josh.

It wasn't as though the touch meant anything. Josh clearly didn't want Mr. Maserati messing with her and was just being his usual protective self, again.

And it wasn't as if she wanted it to mean anything.

Sure, she'd gotten all dolled up this morning, but *not* because she'd wanted Josh to notice her. Because the man had seen her with bedhead!

She had *some* pride.

She slanted a glance at his handsome profile. Okay, maybe she'd hoped he'd notice a smidgen.

As Anne led the way into the sanctuary, Becki remembered why she didn't want to be here. A cheery melody instantly transported her back to Gran's Sunday-school classes.

Becki drew in a fortifying breath. She blinked rapidly and tried to focus on something else. Anything else.

Sunshine gleamed through the windows, splashing rainbows about the room, nothing like the gray day when she'd buried her grandparents.

She avoided making eye contact with those who glanced her way, afraid she wouldn't be able to bear the sympathy in their eyes. She lifted her gaze to the stained-glass image, on the wall behind the pulpit, of Jesus cradling a lamb.

Josh gave her shoulder a reassuring squeeze. "You okay?"

The compassion in his whispered question threatened to undo her. She pulled her gaze away from the image and nodded, but she felt bereft the instant he withdrew his hand.

He motioned toward the back pew. "Let's sit here."

Grateful for his understanding, she quickly took a seat. When he slid in beside her, she snuck a glance at the others still filing in. Her gaze collided with Mr. Maserati.

He smiled, a dimple winking on his cheek.

Josh snorted, then leaned forward and reached for a hymnal, effectively blocking her view of the heartthrob.

On purpose? She shot him a glance.

Looking suspiciously innocent, Josh leaned back and rested his arm on the pew behind her.

He must've done it on purpose. Didn't Josh think she had enough sense not to get taken in by a guy like that?

Before she could decide if she was more irritated or amused, the worship team streamed onto the stage and invited the congregation to stand and sing.

Josh's deep baritone, so much like Gramps's beautiful singing voice, filled her senses, reminding her of the sweet harmonies Gramps and Gran used to sing during the car rides home from church.

A bittersweet ache squeezed her heart. She tried to join in on the chorus, but her voice cracked. Josh's sympathetic glance almost finished her. By sheer willpower, she shifted her mind into Neutral and joined her alto to the array of voices.

After a few songs, the pastor invited everyone to welcome those standing nearby.

Mrs. O'Reilly bustled across the aisle and gave Josh's hand a hearty shake. "Glad to see you're finally taking my advice."

Josh's lips flattened into the polite smile he used to don whenever his aunt Betsy visited, but the woman didn't seem to notice.

She scooped up Becki's hand with a smile as wide as the Mississippi. "Welcome, welcome!"

"Thank you," Becki responded automatically, tugging her gaze from Josh. *What was that all about?*

As the woman continued down the row, Becki glanced around, but she didn't see anything else that might explain Josh's peculiar reaction. "What advice was she talking about?" Becki whispered close to his ear.

He shifted in the pew. "Nothing."

She arched her brow. "Really, *nothing?*"

"Nothing important."

"Maybe you should just go with it," Anne suggested.

"Don't be ridiculous."

"Go with what?" Becki asked.

Ignoring the question, Anne squeezed Josh's arm. "It'd get those ladies off your back."

"It's only once a week. Pretty sure I can handle it, Anne."

"Handle *what?*" Becki interjected.

Bart turned her way and smiled again, diverting her attention.

He really was good-looking. Too bad he had that slick veneer.

At the feel of Josh's arm slipping around her shoulders, her heartbeat went wacky. And it didn't help that he met her puzzled look with that heart-stopping grin.

"On second thought…" He curled his arm a little more tightly around her and turned back to his sister. "That's a great idea."

"See, I told you."

Becki waved her hand in front of them. "*Hello?* What's a great idea?"

"You guys look good together," Anne added, still focused on Josh.

Heat rushed to Becki's face. Then Josh's warm-as-a-summer-meadow eyes captured her gaze, and her cheeks positively flamed.

"Oh, yeah." Anne chuckled. "You guys could totally pull this off."

"What are you two talking about?" Becki scrambled to catch up as her heart did crazy pirouettes.

"Just pretend to be his girlfriend," Anne whispered, motioning them to sit down again. "We'll explain later."

Be his girlfriend? "Seriously?"

Josh gave her a squeeze. "Mrs. O'Reilly drives me crazy with her matchmaking ploys. You'd be doing me a favor."

A favor? A favor.

Of course, because the speed with which he'd backed out of her house that morning should have been her first clue to his true feelings. "You're serious?"

He gave her a take-pity-on-me look.

The music swelled, saving her from responding. Only… the song—"The Old Rugged Cross"—was one of Gran's favorites.

Becki started to sing, but emotions clogged her throat. By the time they reached "Then He'll call me someday to my home far away, where His glory forever I'll share," tears stung her eyes. If only she could know it was true. That Gran and Gramps…

She tried to swallow, tried to forget that she still had the sermon to get through.

Josh reached over and squeezed her hand.

Blinking rapidly, she clung to it, grateful she didn't have to bear the loss alone.

If only the ruse was real.

SIX

What had he been thinking? Josh glanced across the seat of the Cadillac at Bec's far-too-quiet profile. As bad as it sounded, he hoped she was quiet from being emotionally strung out by the service. Not because she was mortified that his sister had wangled her into pretending to be his girlfriend.

He never should have taken up Anne's suggestion—in church, no less—but when he'd seen Winslow tossing Bec that oily smile, he hadn't been able to help himself.

She needed protection from that creep.

Never mind that his heart had felt two sizes too big when she'd clung to his hand through the service or, Lord help him, that his heart sped up at the way her curls escaped her scarf to dance in the breeze. Josh dragged his attention back to the road. No wonder Winslow had tried to catch her eye. Not that he'd appreciate her other qualities—her faith and an appreciation for simple rural living that seemed so hard to find in a woman these days.

Josh tightened his grip on the steering wheel. Maybe he should just put an end to the sham now. From her bewildered *You're serious?* back in the sanctuary, she'd clearly never thought of him as a potential boyfriend.

He'd always been a big brother. A big brother infatuated with her older sister. Which, as he recalled, had irritated Bec more than once when she'd wanted him to play in the woods with her and her menagerie of adopted animals. Then again, if he didn't mention it, the whole thing might be forgotten by next Sunday. It wasn't as if they had to pretend to be an item when no one was looking.

The car hit a bump and jostled Bec into his side.

"You okay?" he said.

She straightened. "Yeah. Just tired."

He gave her a sympathetic glance. She'd tried so hard to contain her grief during the service, but he'd felt her restrained sobs as she clung to his hand.

He was glad he could be there for her. At least some good had come of their ruse.

"The first time back is always the hardest," he said gently. "It'll get easier each week."

Her hands twisted in her lap, and suddenly he feared that she didn't plan on going back.

Hopefully, he could change that. "You still up for an afternoon outing?" He'd promised, and he'd keep that promise if she wanted, but he was also eager to follow up on Netherby's information. Maybe get a look inside the car from the quarry. See if he could find anything more to link it to its owner and Bec's prowler.

"I don't know." She sounded exhausted.

Or was she uncomfortable with the idea of spending time alone with him? "You weren't really interested in Bart Winslow, were you?" Josh pulled into the driveway. "Because I don't want this O'Reilly ruse to mess up any plans you might have to meet men."

She smirked. "Unless the man is Bart, right?"

"Yeah, except for him," Josh quipped, then instantly sobered. "He's the son of the most crooked real-estate broker in the county, and he will stoop to just about anything to help his dear old dad get what he wants."

"So he couldn't possibly be interested in *me*." She climbed from the car.

"I didn't say that." Josh shimmied across the seat to climb out, too. "You just need to know that his motives might not be what they seem."

She dragged her scarf from her hair and squinted at the sun. "It wasn't supposed to be like this."

"What wasn't?"

"Moving to Gran and Gramps's. I'd always felt happy here. Safe. But it's turning into a nightmare."

"We'll catch this guy, Bec. I promise you."

"It's not just that. My sister is doing everything she can to force me to sell. And now you think this real-estate guy's going to start harassing me, too."

"Let's not worry about any of that today, okay? We'll change, grab the picnic basket and the dog, and go for a long ride—enjoy the countryside like your grandparents would have wanted you to."

"Yes," she said, a bit of her enthusiasm returning.

A patrol car pulled to the side of the road in front of the house, and the passenger window opened.

"Be right back," Josh said to Bec and then jogged down the driveway. "You see anyone?" he asked Hunter when he got to the car.

"Afraid I got called away. A camper jackknifed on the highway, caused a pileup."

Josh let out a sigh. "All right. Probably was a long shot anyway. But keep up the patrols if you can."

"Will do." Hunter drove off, and Josh turned back to the house.

The front door stood open. An instant later Bec backed out of the house, her hand splayed over her chest.

Josh raced toward her. "What is it? What's wrong?"

She half turned, her face ashen. "He's here."

Becki twisted her scarf between her fingers and searched the windows. "There's a smell. It's not right." The house was supposed to smell like the perfume Gran dotted on her wrists or her grandfather's Old Spice with maybe a hint of that muscle rub Gran used to massage into his shoulders.

Not the musky odor that had assaulted her senses.

Josh immediately positioned himself between her and the door. "You saw someone?"

"No. I could smell his cologne."

Josh whipped out his phone. "I need you back here now," he barked to the person on the other end. He clipped the phone back onto his belt and squeezed her shoulder. "We'll wait for Hunter."

Hunter's patrol car swung onto the street, its rear end swerving into the opposite lane before righting itself. He parked across the end of the driveway and killed his swirling lights, then jogged toward them. In his uniform, he looked more like a policeman than Rambo, but just as determined. He handed Josh his Taser.

Josh pulled the house key from the lock and tossed it to Hunter. "You take the back."

Becki teetered, but before she could ask what she was supposed to do, Josh grabbed her hand and tugged her behind him. "Stick close."

She welcomed his solid, confident grip and stayed right on his heels. In no time, he'd cleared the front of the house and Hunter the rear.

"Any sign he ran out the back?" Josh asked Hunter.

"Nothing."

"Okay, I'll take the upstairs. You take the basement."

The instant they stepped into the master bedroom, Becki froze. "He's here," she hissed.

Josh sniffed the air and nodded. He motioned her back then stepped to the side of the closet, his Taser raised.

Once again, his gaze connected with hers. *Stay back,* he mouthed, then flung open the closet door.

No one was inside.

No one was anywhere in the room or anywhere else upstairs.

"Are you sure it's not your grandfather's aftershave you're smelling? With the house closed up all morning, you could—"

"No, Gramps always wore Old Spice." She picked up the bottle from the highboy and spritzed the air, fighting tears. "I don't understand. Why'd this guy come in the house if he's after the car?"

Josh pried the bottle from her hand and set it back down. "Maybe you shouldn't touch anything just yet. Can you tell if anything is missing?"

"Not without touching anything."

"Okay, just try to stick to the edges."

She jerked into action, checked the drawers, the closet, Gran's jewelry box, inwardly fuming at the thought of some creep pawing through her grandparents' belongings. But nothing seemed disturbed, let alone missing.

She sank onto the edge of her bed and clasped her head. "Why is God letting this happen?"

Josh hunkered down in front of her. "It's going to be okay, Bec."

"My grandparents were good people."

"They were. But God doesn't promise to spare us from bad circumstances. He only promises to carry us through. You need to trust in Him."

She gave her head a violent shake. "How can I trust a God who let a squirrel build a nest in my grandparents' chimney?"

Josh smoothed her hair and held her gaze with a shared pain that chiseled cracks in the shell around her heart. "Because He loves you, Bec."

She lifted her eyes to the painting on the wall of Jesus cradling a lost lamb —a replica of the church's window. *God cares so much that He comes looking for you when you're lost,* her gran used to say.

In this house, when Gran and Gramps were alive, she used to be able to believe that.

"I didn't imagine that smell," she whispered, stuffing away thoughts of God. "Someone was here."

"Someone was here, all right." Hunter's massive frame filled the doorway.

Josh pushed to his feet. "What did you find?"

"The main-floor bathroom window was pried open."

Becki's anger exploded. "My sister always snuck into the house that way."

"Did you check the cameras?" Josh asked, dismissing her insinuation.

His teenage infatuation with her sister had obviously colored his judgment. Clearly she was behind this.

"Yeah," Hunter said flatly. "They're dead."

"What do you mean, they're dead?"

"Someone tampered with them."

Not her sister, then. Becki lurched to her feet. This was all too unbelievable. "If the guy knew about the cameras, why wouldn't he just rip them off?"

"My guess is that he didn't want you to know he was here." Hunter returned her house key. "If I hadn't checked the cameras closely, I might not have noticed. Would have just figured they weren't triggered."

Josh thrust his fingers through his hair and stared out the window. "So our intruder's no dummy."

Becki looked from Hunter to Josh, her head spinning. "This makes no sense. Yesterday, the guy's trying to scare me. Today, he doesn't want me to know he was here? What does he want?"

"Not sure if yesterday's incident is connected," Hunter said. "But this looks to me like someone's convinced your grandfather made off with those jewels."

"Jewels? What jewels?" Becki's gaze snapped to Josh.

Just in time to catch him flick his finger in a slicing motion across his throat.

"What's he talking about?" she demanded.

Josh lowered his hand. "Nothing."

"I'll...uh...grab the evidence kit." Hunter disappeared down the stairs.

"It's not *nothing*," she ground out, holding on to her patience by a thread. How much more could God possibly throw at her?

"Nothing you need to worry about," Josh said in the soothing tones she'd heard him use on injured animals.

"Hunter just called my grandfather a *jewel thief!*" she said, hearing her own voice edge higher.

"Now, Becki, Hunter didn't—"

"Don't 'now, Becki' me like I'm five years old! And don't touch me!" She whirled from his grasp.

"Watch out!" Josh shouted as Bec's heel caught in the hem of her dress.

She teetered at the top of the stairs, her arms windmilling. He lunged for her but grasped only air.

Bec pitched down the stairs.

He vaulted after her.

Three steps from the bottom, she came to a thudding stop.

"Are you okay?" He dropped to his knees, his hands immediately roaming her limbs for injuries.

She swatted him away, a tear leaking from her eye. "This is your fault."

He sat back on his heels and let out a breath. She couldn't be that hurt if she was scolding him. "Bec, I'm sorry. I didn't believe the incidents could be connected. That's why I didn't tell you."

"Tell me what?" She pushed to her feet. *"Aaah!"*

He caught her by the waist and lifted her weight from her legs. "What is it?"

"My ankle." She made a disgusted noise. "It's okay. I can manage." She grabbed the handrail and, reaching around him, braced her other hand on the wall as if she intended to hop.

"Don't. You'll only make it worse." He scooped her into his arms.

"What do you think you're doing?" She twisted in his hold. "Put me down."

He set her on a kitchen chair. "You're down." He lifted her injured leg to rest on a second chair and slipped off her shoe. "I'll get you some ice."

"I don't want ice. I want an answer."

He poked around in the freezer, searching for answers as much as ice. The only thing he knew for sure was that with the daggers shooting from Bec's eyes, Mrs. O'Reilly wouldn't mistake them for a couple a second time. Not that he cared what Mrs. O'Reilly thought; he just wanted Bec to know she could trust him.

Josh pulled a bag of frozen peas from the freezer, wrapped it in a towel and gently laid it across her ankle.

Hunter reappeared with the evidence kit and peered over his shoulder. "What happened?"

"She fell down the stairs." Josh had never seen an ankle swell so fast.

"Looks like you're going to have to take her to the hospital."

Bec folded her arms over her chest. "I'm not going anywhere until I get answers. Why would anyone think my grandparents stole jewels?"

Hunter hitched his thumb over his shoulder. "I'll check that bathroom window for fingerprints."

"Yeah, thanks." *For nothing.* Josh sank into a chair opposite Bec. "Some valuable jewelry was stolen from a museum during your grandparents' last tour."

"You can't possibly think they'd have anything to do with that."

"No, I don't. But when the police learned that your grandparents had left the tour early, they became suspicious. Only—" A lump caught in his throat as he whispered, "It was too late to question them."

She went white. "You think they were murdered?"

"No." Josh stroked the hair from her face, needing to touch her, draw her back. "No, Bec. Your grandparents' deaths were an accident. Believe me, that's the first thing I triple-checked."

She dropped her hands to her lap, suddenly looking way too vulnerable for his peace of mind. "Do you think Hunter could be right about someone looking for the jewelry here?"

"I don't know. Someone might have heard about the police's suspicions. They didn't have enough evidence to secure a search warrant, so maybe your intruder figured he'd look himself."

Bec shook her head. "No would-be thief would go to all this trouble on a far-fetched hunch."

"That's why I didn't mention it yesterday. But now…I'm not so sure."

"No." She straightened. "You were right yesterday. It's probably Neil who's trying to scare me. That's got to be it." She sniffed. "This cologne kind of smells like something he'd wear."

Josh pushed open the kitchen window. As much as he'd like nothing better than to pin all of this on Neil, she was clearly grasping at anything that would divert suspicion from any connection to her grandparents and the jewelry. "We've already concluded that Neil wasn't the driver of the green Plymouth I spotted the night you were hit. He doesn't fit Netherby's description, remember?"

Hunter returned with the fingerprint kit. "Did you say her attacker drove a green Plymouth?"

"Yeah."

"He was here yesterday." Hunter turned to Bec. "That guy you had coffee with."

Josh jerked his gaze to Bec. "Why didn't you tell me?"

"I didn't know Henry's car was a Plymouth. Besides, he couldn't be my attacker. He was a friend of my grandparents'."

Josh expelled a breath. Why was he only finding out now that she'd had a visitor, let alone that he might be their man? "Does he match Netherby's description?"

"Sure, I guess. But it can't be Henry."

"Why not?"

"He gave me his phone number...." Her voice trailed off.

"Where is it?"

She pointed toward the phone.

Josh looked at the paper. Henry Smith. An alias if he'd ever heard one. "Dust this for fingerprints, will you, Hunter?" Except if this guy had been here yesterday, then his car wasn't the one they'd towed from the quarry.

Didn't matter. Josh wasn't about to take any chances where Bec's safety was concerned.

Bec smoothed her skirt, but he didn't miss the way she trembled.

Safety, *right*. He'd utterly failed to protect her already. The cameras hadn't worked. Someone had gotten into the house. What if she'd been home?

She was right. Her life had turned into a nightmare.

If he didn't catch this guy soon, she'd hightail it back to the city long before winter. He should probably encourage her to do just that. She'd be safer.

Except how could he be sure if she was fifty miles away?

SEVEN

Monday afternoon, Becki scrolled through images on the library computer. Images of the jewelry her grandparents were suspected of stealing. Images of diamond-and-ruby earrings, monogrammed cuff links, cameo broaches and much more. She grabbed scratch paper from beside the computer and jotted down the names of the witnesses who'd been interviewed in the online article.

The bold lettering of the classified ads sitting next to her elbow drew her attention back to what she was supposed to be doing—finding a job. If not for her idea of coming to the library to search for one, Josh would probably have a cop babysitting her this very minute.

From the inquisitive glances Mrs. O'Reilly slanted her way every few minutes, Becki half wondered if the older woman was secretly on Josh's payroll, not a library volunteer as she claimed.

Her thoughts drifted back to the web article once more. She shook her head. How many times would she do this?

She had to focus, and not on the suspicions hanging over her grandparents' heads. She should be leaving that to the professionals...to Josh, who believed in her grandparents as much as she did.

She looked down at the scratch paper in her hands and

worked to flatten the crumpled edges. Maybe her grandparents were friends with some of the witnesses.

Stop it. She turned again to the classified ads, but after skimming her finger over several without a word sinking in, she set the newspaper aside and pulled Gran's address book from her purse.

She searched for the names she'd jotted down from the article, but she didn't find a single match. *Now what?*

"Are you still using that computer?" the librarian asked.

"Yes." Becki launched an online search for the contact information of each witness.

Hopefully, these folks would be more helpful than the president of the antique-car club had been when she'd called him earlier. He'd asked more questions than he'd answered and had refused to give the name of a single friend of her grandparents' that she might call.

She would have tried Henry first if Josh hadn't taken his number. She couldn't believe he was a thief. He'd made no attempt to invite himself inside. Well, except for asking about Gran's costumes. But when she'd first invited him to stay for coffee, he'd declined. If he'd been looking for stolen jewelry, wouldn't he have jumped at her invitation?

The two people from Gran's address book she'd managed to connect with hadn't been touring friends, although they would have happily talked to her all day if she hadn't begged off.

If she could just talk to someone who'd been with her grandparents, she was sure she could figure out if there was anything to Josh's jewelry-theft theory. It made far more sense that someone would come after the Cadillac. Maybe when the prowler had seen the car was gone, he'd simply checked out the empty house on a whim.

She clicked back to the newspaper article and studied the photograph of one of the stolen pieces—a double-chained necklace with large gemstones embedded in elaborate filigree dangling from the lower chain. She sure hadn't seen anything like that in Gran's jewelry box.

What was she thinking?

Of course she hadn't. Gran and Gramps would never have stolen jewelry. Anyone who knew them would know that. So if whoever had been prowling around the place hoped to find the loot, he couldn't possibly know them.

In fact, the more she thought about it, the more ridiculous the whole theory seemed.

She shook her head. Would she rather believe her sister and brother-in-law had sent an intruder into the house?

She clicked back to the online directory and managed to track down numbers for three of the witnesses. Phone numbers in hand, she wedged the crutches they'd given her at the hospital last night under her armpits and hobbled outside to make the calls in private.

As she reached her car, another pulled to the curb behind her. "What do you think you're doing?" Josh called through his open window, sounding none too happy.

Becki opened her car door, tossed her purse inside, then repositioned the crutch under her arm so she could turn to face him without putting weight on her injured foot. "Can't a girl take a break?" She swallowed at the sight of him climbing out of a patrol car in his police uniform, looking so tall and handsome and protective. He'd been incredibly attentive at the hospital last night, keeping her company through the long hours they'd had to wait for the doctor to come in and confirm her injury was a sprain.

"Sure." He closed the distance between them in three long strides. "If you were *actually* job hunting."

"Of course I'm job hunting. If I hope to afford to stay in the house, I will need one."

"Uh-huh."

She teetered on her crutches. Did he have someone spying on her in the library?

He cupped her elbow, steadying her. "Your ankle won't get better if you don't rest it."

She tossed her crutches into the backseat, feeling way too much like another one of his broken-winged sparrows or three-legged dogs, even if it was kind of sweet that he worried about her.

Josh shook his head, looking utterly exasperated.

"What?"

"We just got a call at the station from the detective investigating the museum theft."

"You did! What'd he say?"

Josh's stern expression shared none of her excitement. "Seems the president of the antique-car club that hosted the tour talked to a *person of interest*." Josh's gaze grew uncomfortably intense. "You wouldn't happen to know anything about that, would you?"

"Oh." She ducked her head. *Wait a minute.* "They think I had something to do with it?"

"They did until I explained the situation." The exasperation—yes, definitely exasperation—etched on Josh's face bit at her conscience.

"I couldn't just do nothing."

His gaze tracked up one side of the street and down the other. "Interfering with a police investigation isn't helping."

"I wasn't interfering. I just wanted to talk to someone who'd been on the tour with Gran and Gramps. Find out what they'd seen or heard."

"And if your prowler catches word that you're asking too many questions, what do you think he's going to do? Not call the station, you can be sure of that."

Becki couldn't help it. She grinned.

"What are you smiling about?" Josh growled. "This is serious."

"You're not really mad at me. You're *worried* about me."

"Of course I'm worried." He strode back to his car.

"Josh, don't be mad," she called after him, fearing he'd leave in a huff.

He didn't respond, just opened the back door and reached inside.

A floppy-eared dog soared to the sidewalk and bounded toward her, straining at the leash Josh held.

"Oh," she gasped. The tongue-lolling mixed breed, with his mismatched patches of brown-and-black fur and white belly and feet, looked just like the pooch she'd had for a short time as a child.

She knelt and offered him her hand.

The dog gave her a slobbery kiss instead.

Josh laughed. "I guess that answers that question."

"What question?" Becki scratched the dog's neck.

"Whether you want Bruiser."

Her heart leaped. "He's for me?"

"If you want him. He's had his basic obedience training. One of the guys on the force needed to find him a new home after his daughter developed allergies."

"Oh, I'd love to give Bruiser a home." She threw her arms around the pooch and gave him a giant hug. "But such a tough-guy name won't do, will it?" she crooned. "I'll call you…Ruffles."

"Ruffles?" Josh tugged back on the leash. "You're not serious?"

Becki pursed her lips to try to maintain a straight face.

"C'mon, no self-respecting dog should have to endure being called Ruffles."

She laughed. "I knew you'd say that."

He offered her a hand up and held her gaze for a long moment.

She squirmed under the intensity, even as a thrill rushed through her chest.

"You can call him whatever you like. I want you to be happy here." His voice turned husky. "And safe."

Oh. Safe. Right. She tightened her fingers around the piece of paper containing the names and numbers she'd found. What would her prowler do if he learned she was asking questions?

Josh would be furious if she called the witnesses now. But if the news that she'd talked to the club president had gotten to Josh so quickly, maybe the idea that someone had heard of the cops' suspicions of her grandparents wasn't so far-fetched.

"Are you okay with me going home now?" she asked, since he'd been so sweet.

The muscles in his jaw flexed. "If you promise to call at the first sign of any trouble," he said finally, when he clearly wanted to say no. "Deal?"

"Deal." As she reached for the dog leash, Mrs. O'Reilly ambled out the library doors.

"Mighty fine day, isn't it?" the woman chimed, throwing Josh a meaningful look.

Becki struggled to contain the new grin that sprang to her lips. She gave Josh a sideways hug and leaned her head against his chest as she let the grin loose. "Oh, yes! Look at the dog Josh brought me."

Becki reached for the leash, but Josh caught her hand in his and held it fast as his other arm slipped around her waist.

Mrs. O'Reilly glanced from the dog to Josh, her eyes sparkling. "Yes, mighty fine," she repeated and moseyed on up the street.

Becki immediately tried to pull away, but Josh's arm cinched tighter around her waist.

His gaze dropped to hers, a dare flaring to life. "You set me up."

She slipped her hand from his clasp and splayed her fingers over her chest with wide-eyed innocence. "I was just trying to help your cause. Let her believe you're interested. Isn't that what you wanted?"

"My cause, huh?" Light danced in his eyes. "Like the time you came up with the scheme to get your sister to notice me?"

"How was I supposed to know a family of skunks lived under that log? Besides, it worked, didn't it?"

He let her go and gave her a what-am-I-going-to-do-with-you shake of his head. "Oh, yeah, Sarah could smell me coming from a mile away." Josh opened the back door of her car and shooed the dog inside. "You haven't changed a bit, Bec. Still trouble with a capital *T*."

Becki glanced in the rearview mirror at Bruiser sprawled across her backseat. "Josh probably got you for me just so I'd go home and stay out of trouble."

Bruiser yowled.

Trouble with a capital *T*. Was that what Josh really thought of her?

Considering all that had happened around here since she'd arrived, she supposed she couldn't blame him. So she should just stop thinking about how handsome he looked in that police uniform, let alone how at home she'd felt in his arms.

Oh, yes, she definitely needed to forget about that.

Josh would never make a home with someone who didn't share his faith, and her outburst about the squirrels' nest had left little question about the shaky state of hers.

She pulled the car into her driveway and opened the back door to grab her crutches. "Here you go, Bruiser. Your new home. Hope you like it."

Bruiser bounded from the car without a second's hesitation and took off around the house.

So much for basic obedience. She supposed the phone calls would have to wait until after she got Bruiser settled. She grabbed her crutches. Before she reached the corner, Bruiser let out a low-pitched growl that sent a chill down her arms.

"Good dog" came a frightened male voice.

Becki ducked. There was only one reason why a strange man would sneak around her house. But he didn't sound like Henry. She edged closer to the corner as she fumbled for her phone. The hot sun glinted off a motorcycle parked behind the house. A big, shiny black bike. The kind of bike that scary-looking biker-gang dudes drove.

"Nice boy," the man repeated inanely between Bruiser's unrelenting growls.

Okay, maybe not a gang biker.

"Hello," he called out. "Anyone there? Name's Winslow, the real-estate agent." His voice pitched higher as if that should explain everything.

"Bart?" He didn't sound like Mr. Maserati.

"No, his father. Please call off your dog."

Becki's thumb hovered over the connect button for Josh's number. He was never going to see her as grown-up if she kept calling him to her rescue. "What are you doing here?" Becki asked without stepping into the man's line of sight.

"Albert Graw's granddaughter asked me to appraise the place."

Becki's fingers tightened around the handle of her crutch. She rounded the corner of the house. "You're lying."

The man took a step toward her, but Bruiser's growling immediately intensified.

Way to go, Bruiser!

The man's arms shot into the air. "I'm not. I swear." He wore a suit jacket, despite the heat and his apparent mode of transportation. Sweat beaded his forehead, pooling at his bushy eyebrows and dripping in tiny rivulets down his pudgy cheeks. "She called my office this morning. Asked me to meet her here at two."

Becki glanced at her watch. "Well, it's two. I'm here. And guess what? I didn't call you."

"You're Graw's granddaughter?"

"Yes."

His brows drew together. "Well, someone called me." He reached inside his jacket, and the dog lunged. The man's hand snapped back into view, a business card between his fingers.

Bruiser backed up, but he added a bark for good measure.

Becki hid a smile. She loved the dog already.

"Could you please call off your dog? If you don't want a valuation, I'll go, but I'm telling you the truth. Does Mr. Graw have another granddaughter, perhaps?"

Becki's heart dropped. Sarah wouldn't. Yes, she would. Becki squinted at the man. "She said she'd meet you here?"

"Yes."

As if on cue, her sister's BMW rolled into the driveway.

Becki swung her crutches around and loped toward her sister's car.

"Hey, what about your dog?" the real-estate agent cried out after her.

"Bruiser, come here," Becki called over her shoulder, having no clue whether the dog would actually listen. "We have another culprit to corner," she muttered and braced herself as Sarah stepped from the car.

Bruiser raced around the corner, grazing his chin on the gravel as his legs went out from under him on the curve. But without losing a step he barreled right for Becki and took up sentry duty at her side.

Sarah arched a perfectly plucked eyebrow at the canine. Then, before Becki's eyes, Sarah's crusty facade crumbled. "He looks just like Max!" She squatted and ruffled the dog's ears. "Where did you find him?"

The wistful expression on her sister's face melted Becki's anger. They'd always been the best of friends as children, and never more so than the weeks after Dad gave away their beloved Max.

A man's voice jarred her back to the present. "You are the other granddaughter, I presume," the real-estate agent said, standing well back as he eyed Bruiser.

Sarah sprang to her feet, her gaze skittering past Becki to the agent. "Yes." Her face flushed.

"And she had no right to call you," Becki added. "I own this property, and I have no intention of selling."

"Most city folk say the same when they first move here, until they have to deal with the inevitable problems—annoying critters, leaky roofs, contaminated wells, not to mention the isolation. Then their idealistic view changes pretty quick." The man ventured closer, stiffening at Bruiser's growl, and handed Becki his card. "This is how to reach me if you change your mind. Summer is a better time to sell. These old places get drafty in winter. Expensive to heat, too." He strode toward his motorcycle.

"Wait," Sarah cried out. "I want to know how much the place could sell for."

"At least two hundred thousand," the man said, then kicked up his motorcycle stand and roared away.

"I guess now that you got what you came for, you'll be going." Becki turned toward the house and the phone calls she needed to make.

Sarah hurried after her. "Actually, I came to help you."

"Help me?"

"Yes. You can't clean and get settled in with that sore ankle. I can't believe you didn't call me."

Becki stopped. "That's right, I didn't. So how did you find out?"

A flower-delivery van pulled into the driveway.

At least, those were the words emblazoned across the side. Becki willed herself not to imagine gunmen pouring out the back of the van to mow her down. Stuff like that only happened in the movies.

The driver jumped down from the truck, carrying a colorful assortment of flowers. "One of you ladies Rebecca Graw?"

"Yes, that's me." Becki lifted her hand as she gaped at the spectacular bouquet. Who would send her flowers?

The man eyed her crutches and hesitated.

"I'll take them for her," Sarah volunteered, and the man handed them over.

Becki hopped closer to her sister to get a look at the card. "Who are they from?"

Sarah pulled out the card. "Neil. He wrote, 'Sorry to hear about your fall. Hope you get well soon.'"

Dread sank like a rock to the pit of Becki's stomach. "How'd he find out?"

She didn't realize she'd asked the question aloud until her sister answered.

"Probably the same way I did. From your former room-mate. I can't believe you'd call her and not your own sister."

"I didn't call anyone. She happened to call while I was at the hospital." Becki left the *If you called once in a while...* unsaid. The only reason her sister called lately was to harass her into selling. Becki's glance snapped to Sarah. "What prompted you to call my roommate?"

"I didn't. She posted a prayer request for you on her Facebook page. Then when I tried to call the house, there was no answer."

"Oh." Becki wanted to believe genuine concern had prompted her sister's trip, but the real-estate agent's presence said otherwise. More likely she'd jumped at the excuse to scope out the place to compile more ammunition to give her lawyers, or lawyer husband, to force her out, which reminded Becki that she'd forgotten to call Gramps's lawyer today.

Sarah grabbed a small suitcase from her trunk. "Rowan said I could stay as long as you need me."

"As long as it takes to convince me to sell, you mean." Becki plowed toward the house on her crutches.

Sarah didn't respond.

Becki halted at the porch steps and faced her sister. "You don't deny it?"

"That's not why I'm here," she said quietly, her inability

to look Becki in the eye denying every word. "But yes, it's why Rowan let me come."

"He *let* you, huh? As if you ever ask permission to do anything you want to." Becki let out a snort. But as she whirled to hop up the porch steps, she thought she saw tears in her sister's eyes.

Once inside, Sarah headed straight for the kitchen, pulled a vase from the corner cupboard and arranged the flowers in it. "You were smart not to marry Neil."

"He never asked."

"Because you were smart enough to get out of the relationship before then."

Becki plugged in the kettle, then leaned against the counter and stared at her sister. "I thought you liked Neil. He's a lot like your Rowan."

An indefinable emotion flashed in Sarah's eyes before she glanced away, busying herself with the flowers. "But you're not like me. You were never obsessed with getting things."

Becki's grip on the crutches tightened. "I'm not giving up the house, Sarah."

"That's not what I meant."

"Isn't it?" Becki hated how petty she sounded. But Sarah had already admitted that Rowan had urged her to come here to convince Becki to sell. For all she knew, he was behind the attacks, too. "The value of this house to me can't be measured in dollars. So you might as well call off Rowan and his goons, because I'm not selling."

"Goons? What are you talking about?" Sarah set the vase on the center of the table and then tugged her long sleeves back to her wrists, gripping them with trembling fingers, as if she knew *exactly* what Becki was talking about.

And in that moment, Becki knew she wouldn't need to make those phone calls, because Josh's jewelry-theft theory was wrong.

"I'm talking about the creep who broke into my house, who

clobbered me with a two-by-four, who—" she snatched up the note she'd found in her mailbox the day she'd arrived and slapped it into Sarah's hand "—wants me out of this house."

Sarah gaped at the words. "I…" She shook her head. "You think Rowan did all that?"

"You're the only one who'd benefit from scaring me out of this place."

"But this isn't Rowan's writing. I can't believe…" Sarah's gaze shifted away.

"You can't believe what? That he'd stoop so low?"

EIGHT

Outside the pet-food store, Josh tossed a bag of dog food and two dishes into the cab of his truck, grateful for an excuse to check on Bec. He yanked the truck door closed with a snort. If he was smart, he'd go home and keep a protective watch from afar.

She'd been all smiles and hugs after he sprang Bruiser on her. He'd gotten a kick out of watching her. She'd looked like an excited little kid as the dog slobbered over her face. But that hug—the one she'd given him for Mrs. O'Reilly's benefit—hadn't felt like a kid's hug at all.

Worse than that, he'd wanted it to be real.

Except he wasn't so sure anymore if she shared his faith. Never mind that another incident like yesterday's break-in was bound to drive her back to the city faster than he could say goodbye.

He peered through the windshield at the darkening sky. A gust of wind whipped the tree limbs into a frenzy. Looked as if they were in for a bad storm. Which made for the kind of night most people would hole up at home. Hopefully, Bec's prowler was one of them, because so far Josh hadn't tracked down a single Henry Smith that matched their suspect's description. Not that he'd had a lot of opportunity. As far as his captain was concerned, there was no case to investigate.

He stepped on the gas, hoping to beat the storm. Two

miles from home—far too close for comfort—Josh spotted a green Plymouth.

He called dispatch. "Can you pull up the vehicle registration for…" He rattled off the license plate and a minute later had confirmation he'd found his man.

Now if only he were driving a patrol car, he could flash his lights, blip his siren and force the guy to pull over.

Instead he hung back to see if Smith would head for Bec's.

Sure enough, he turned onto their street and a moment later slowed in front of Bec's house.

Yes. If Smith pulled in, Josh would have him.

A second later, Smith sped off.

Josh sped up enough to keep Smith in sight and called Hunter. "You still in a black-and-white?"

"Yeah."

"I spotted Smith. Headed west on Elm. I'm—" Josh caught sight of a black BMW in Bec's driveway and hit the brakes. "Haul him in for me, will you? I'll be down as soon as I can." He clicked off and swerved into Bec's driveway, praying he wouldn't regret not taking time for reconnaissance first.

The Toronto dealer's logo on the trunk of the car suggested the car's owner could be another one of her city friends come to lure her back or a developer trying to sweet-talk her into selling.

Both possibilities made him want to punch something, but at this point, either would be better than option three.

He shoved the bag of dog food under his arm and grabbed the pair of bowls. If she wouldn't even agree to move out for a few days while he tracked down her intruder, some flashy BMW driver wouldn't convince her to sell. She was too determined to hang on to the old place.

Thunder rumbled in the distance.

Josh strode to the back door, scanning the windows. Two figures moved about the kitchen. Both female. A friend, then. He let out his pent-up breath and knocked.

Sarah opened the door.

For a second he stood speechless. *You're the last person I expected to see here* didn't seem like a neighborly thing to say. She looked as perfectly put together as she had at the funeral, but from the amount of gunk caked around her eyes, clearly her vanity battled aging in daily combat.

Her gaze dropped to the bag under his arm, and she pushed the door wide. "Great timing. We were just wondering what we'd feed Bruiser."

A chair scraped the floor. Bec sank into the seat, a pained expression pinching her face.

Josh handed Sarah the dog dishes and squatted beside Bec. "Are you okay? Is the ankle worse?"

Her gaze slid to her sister. "No, I'm fine." She sounded defeated. Not fine at all.

Bruiser positioned himself between them as if Josh was the one she needed protection from.

Josh searched her face, but her expression had blanked.

How dare her sister come here and harangue her into giving up their grandparents' home?

Sarah filled one of the dog dishes with water. "Can I make you some coffee?"

"Thanks, but no. I can't stay," he said, not taking his eyes from Bec. "I've got a lead on Smith," he whispered for her ears only, then ruffled the dog's fur before standing.

A bouquet of flowers on the table snagged his attention. He tilted his head to peek at the card, then wished he hadn't.

"Oh, yuck. What is that smell?" Sarah wrinkled her nose.

Bec mimicked her sister's disgusted expression. "Gross. It smells like rotten eggs. Did it come from the fridge?"

Josh sniffed the air. "Could be sulfur in your water." He turned on the tap Sarah had just used, and the smell intensified. "Oh, yeah, you've got sulfur in your well, all right."

"Since when? I don't ever remembering smelling that when I visited."

Josh shook his head. "No, I can't remember your grandparents ever complaining about it. But last summer a few houses around here were suddenly struck with it. It's usually worse after a heavy rain." He glanced out the window at the storms piling up on the horizon. "Not before."

Sarah pinched her nostrils. "That must be what the real-estate agent meant about people moving back to the city. How could anyone stand living with that smell?"

Josh clenched his jaw. "Winslow?" He directed the question to Bec. He should've expected Bart and his dad wouldn't waste any time swooping in on the place.

"Yeah. He was here when I got home." Becki patted Bruiser's head. "But Bruiser let him know how we feel about real-estate agents. Didn't you, fella?"

A sentiment Sarah, no doubt, didn't share. "What brings you here, Sarah?" Josh asked.

She stopped holding her nose and cracked open the bag of dog food. "I came to help out my little sister until her ankle gets better."

Bec's lips pursed at the "little" modifier.

Josh wondered if she believed her sister's story. "I'm sure she'll appreciate the company. She tell you I'm a police officer now?"

Sarah set down the dish and turned abruptly toward him. "No, I thought you took over the farm."

"Yeah, I still live next door. It's given me a firsthand view of the trouble someone's been giving Bec. You know anything about that?"

"No. I already told Bec I don't."

"But you do want her to sell the place?" He wasn't sure what compelled him to push, considering Henry looked like their man.

Sarah folded her arms over her chest and pierced Josh with a glare. "That's between Bec and me. I don't see what business it is of yours."

Whoa, talk about striking a nerve. Josh's cell phone rang. He checked the screen. "Excuse me, I need to take this."

"You're going to want to get down here," Hunter said the instant Josh connected.

"Is Henry our man?"

"Yes and no."

"What do you mean?"

"Just get down here."

Josh darted through the pelting rain into the police station. The glare of fluorescents intensified the throb that had started in his head the second Hunter had called. He shook the water from his jacket.

"You're too late." Hunter's sour expression sent a chill through Josh that had nothing to do with the deluge outside. "The captain let Smith go. Wants to see you in his office."

"Let him go?" Josh stormed into the captain's office without knocking. "What's going on?"

Hunter leaned against the doorpost, arms crossed over his chest.

The captain stepped out from behind his desk and hitched his hip onto the corner, an action that made him seem a fraction more open-minded than the persona exuded by his severe crew cut, crisply pressed uniform and powerful build. "Hunter fill you in?"

"Said you let Smith go. Why? I can place this guy at the scene the night of the first attack."

"Calm down." The captain patted the air. "Smith is a P.I. The museum hired him to investigate the jewelry theft."

Josh jerked his gaze to Hunter. "That's his story?"

Hunter shrugged. "It checked out."

"Okay—" Josh swung back to the captain "—so he's a P.I. That doesn't give him license to trespass in the Graws' barn and clobber Miss Graw over the head with a two-by-four."

"Smith said another guy was in the barn. He saw him sneak

across the field as he drove by. It's what made him pull into the farm lane."

"Sounds like a convenient alibi to me. He give you a description?"

The captain put on his reading glasses and pulled a paper from his desk. "Wore a dark hooded sweatshirt. Couldn't see any of his features."

"Lot of help that is."

"Look." The captain set down the paper and removed his glasses. "The fact is, we don't have enough resources to keep this up. Smith doesn't think the Graws had any connection to the heist, so there's no reason to think anyone else would."

"Someone's still terrorizing her." And despite Sarah's defensive reaction to his questions, Josh couldn't believe she was behind this. He paced to the window and squinted into the blackness.

"Terrorizing? She surprised someone in her barn. Now you think everything else is connected, like that car you fished out of the quarry. A car dumped by some guy cleaning out his back forty. Don't you think you might be letting your emotions cloud your judgment here?"

"No." Josh squashed the memory of his annoyance at those flowers from Neil. Bec was a neighbor who needed his help. Nothing more. "She's a citizen of Serenity who deserves our protection."

"She's got a police officer living next door." The captain pushed off the desk and returned to his seat. "That's going to have to do. She's not the only citizen in this town."

"But—"

The captain motioned to the door. "Go home. And don't call any more personnel in on this. Hunter and Wes are not your personal commando team."

Josh stalked out of the office with Hunter on his six. "Can you believe him?"

Hunter made a weird cluck and gave him a look like, yeah, he could.

Josh threw him a scowl.

"Hey, you've got to admit you get a little obsessed."

"Hardly."

"Man, you have a three-legged dog and a bird with a broken wing. If something or someone needs rescuing, you're the go-to guy."

Josh snorted. "Get real." If he'd been the least bit obsessive, the Graws wouldn't have died of carbon-monoxide poisoning.

He needed to get back to Bec. For all he knew, Smith could be on his way there now.

A scream. Her sister's scream yanked Becki out of a deep sleep—the deepest she'd had since arriving in Serenity, which was a little unnerving considering that she was the only person that stood between her sister and more than half of their grandparents' estate.

"Becki!" Sarah shouted again, jolting Becki thoroughly awake.

The dog barked and howled, prancing back and forth from Becki's bed to the closed bedroom door.

Becki grabbed her bathrobe and hopped to the door. The instant she opened it, Bruiser raced out. Becki squinted at the sudden change in light.

Sarah dashed from the bathroom to her bedroom, her arms loaded with bath towels. "The roof's leaking."

"I'll go down and get a bucket."

Sarah glanced at Becki's bandaged ankle and unloaded the towels into her arms. "Better let me get the buckets." Sarah dashed down the stairs, turning every light on as she went. Bruiser raced after her.

Becki hobbled toward the bedroom, grateful her sister was there tonight even if Becki doubted her true motives for coming were as pure as she'd let on. Sarah had gotten too tight-lipped after Becki alleged Rowan was behind the trouble she'd been having.

Before she dared leave Sarah alone in the house, Becki needed to figure out why her sister was really here. Josh might think Henry was her attacker, but like he'd said, Sarah still wanted the house sold. And as much as Becki didn't want to believe her sister would stoop to any means to make that happen, she wasn't so sure anymore.

Becki turned into the bedroom, and the towels spilled from her arms. "No!"

Above the bed, the plaster bulged. Every couple of seconds, a giant water drop plopped onto the pillow below. Becki wedged herself between the head of the bed and the wall and shoved.

Sarah ran back into the room, carrying two big pots. "What are you doing?"

"Saving the bed."

"You're going to hurt yourself." Sarah moved in beside her, and they shoved the bed out of the way. "Okay, lay down some towels to catch the splash, and we'll set the pots on top."

Rain thrashed the window, and the drops from the ceiling came faster. Becki positioned a pot beneath them. "I can't believe I slept through this storm."

"At the rate it's pouring, that plaster might not hold."

The concern in her sister's voice surprised Becki. She would have thought Sarah would latch onto this disaster as one more reason she should sell. Sarah certainly had continued to make a big deal about that horrid sulfur smell long after Josh had left.

Sarah passed her the second pot, and Becki gasped at the sight of her face.

Sarah's hand sprang to cover the bruise around her unmade-up eye.

"What happened?"

"I...I walked into the door, trying to find the light switch. Is it that bad?"

Becki squinted at the yellowing mark. "That didn't just happen." Her gaze skittered to similar marks on Sarah's arms.

Sarah must have noticed, because she immediately dropped her hand and tugged down the sleeves of her pajama top.

"How did you get those bruises?"

"I don't know what you're talking about."

"I'm talking about this." Becki grabbed Sarah's arm and shoved up her sleeve.

Sarah shrank back.

Becki stared at her sister, her beautiful sister, and felt sick and utterly ashamed. "Did Rowan..."

"I'm fine." Sarah fussed with the towels.

Becki threw her arms around her sister. "Oh, Sarah, I'm sorry. I didn't know. You should have told me." Here she'd been thinking such horrible thoughts about her sister when she'd really come here to escape her husband. Had Josh guessed?

Was that why he'd stared at Sarah so long when she'd first opened the door?

Becki had thought he was still infatuated...

Sarah remained stiff, sucking in air in short bursts. "It's not what you think. It was my fault."

Pounding erupted at the back door. Bruiser set off barking again and tore down the stairs.

"Bec, what's going on?" Josh's shout pierced the window-pane above the sound of the storm raging outside, which was nothing compared to the rage Becki felt toward her brother-in-law at the moment.

Sarah pulled away and tugged her sleeves back down. "You can't say anything. Please. Promise me." She grabbed her makeup bag and long-sleeved shirt and darted into the bathroom.

Downstairs, Josh sounded as if he might take down the door any second. And the dog's constant howling didn't help.

Gritting her teeth against the pain in her ankle, Becki raced down the stairs as fast as she could. "Quiet, Bruiser." She unlocked the dead bolt and, before she could twist the doorknob, Josh pushed through the door.

"What's going on? I saw all the lights come on and your phone's dead."

Becki took one look at the worry etched on his face and flung herself into his arms.

He drew her close, his heart hammering beneath her ear. "What's wrong? What happened?"

Coming to her senses, she reluctantly pushed away from him. "I can't tell you."

He caught her with a gentle hand at the back of her neck and whisked a tear from her cheek, the compassion in his eyes so heartfelt she yearned to step back into the shelter of his arms.

"The roof's leaking," Sarah said tersely from the kitchen doorway.

Becki jerked from Josh's grasp. Whoa, how had Sarah put herself together so quickly?

Josh's gaze ping-ponged between them, as if he'd sensed the underlying warning Sarah had sent Becki's way. His gaze stalled on her, waiting.

"The plaster's bulging. I'm afraid it might give way."

He nodded but looked far from satisfied. "I'll take a look. I might be able to throw up a tarp temporarily to ward off any more damage until the rain stops."

"I can't ask you to do that. It's pouring out there."

"You didn't. I offered. Which room is it?"

"I'll show you." Sarah led him upstairs.

Becki slipped into the downstairs bathroom and splashed water on her face. She never used to lose it so easily. But she'd been overwhelmed by the realization that Sarah's husband had beat her—she hadn't been able to help herself when she saw the concern in Josh's expression.

"Bec?" Josh called from the kitchen.

Becki dried her face and shook her head at the mess of curls in her reflection. Couldn't be helped. Rejoining Josh, she looked around. "Where's Sarah?"

"Upstairs changing the bedsheets." He stepped closer. "What did she say to upset you like that?"

Becki swallowed at the tenderness in his voice, at his concern for her, *not* her sister. But she held her emotions in check. "Nothing."

His head tilted. "*Nothing?* That sounds familiar."

She smiled at his teasing.

He caught a strand of her hair and twirled it around his finger. "Do you think she had that real-estate agent punch a few holes in the roof to convince you to sell?"

She chuckled. "Sounds like something I might've thought a few hours ago. But I was wrong about her."

Josh searched her eyes, and the change in his expression made Becki wonder if he could see right inside her head and read her thoughts. He'd learn the truth soon enough after she invited her sister to stay. He dropped his hand. "I'll see if I can jury-rig a temporary fix on the roof."

"Be careful, Josh, please. I don't want to see you get hurt on my account."

His lips quirked into a quick smile, and he pressed an equally quick kiss to her forehead. A kiss that made her feel like a kid who'd needed rescuing again.

Not the cared-about woman she'd felt like when she'd stepped into his arms. How was he ever going to believe she could take care of herself if she kept letting him run to her rescue every time anything remotely bad happened?

As he slipped out the door, Sarah rejoined her in the kitchen. "He's grown up to be a really nice guy."

Becki watched his flashlight bob in the darkness. "He was

always someone you could count on." She drew in a deep breath and mentally rehearsed her invitation for Sarah to stay.

Sarah stepped closer to the door and watched Josh, too. "I guess I would've been better off waiting for *him* all those years ago."

Becki touched her forehead where Josh had kissed her. If Sarah stayed, would Josh...

Becki's invitation turned to paste in her mouth.

NINE

Rain lashed Josh's back as he muscled the ladder through the barn door.

You've got to admit you get a little obsessed.

Dropping the ladder inside the pitch-black building, he shut out Hunter's voice. He wasn't obsessed. Any decent human being would have put up that tarp for Bec.

A rustle sounded from the far corner of the barn.

He swung his LED light that way. The beam picked up a light-colored trail of tiny pebbles. He bent to take a closer look. Not pebbles. Tiny yellow bits. He picked up a couple and brought them to his nose. Sulfur.

He should have guessed. He traced his light along the trail. Another rustle. He flicked his light toward the sound, but the light blinked out. He slapped it against his leg, toggled the switch. Nothing worked.

The door banged closed.

He ducked behind a bench.

"Whew, that's some wind." Bec's flashlight beam bounced around the walls. "Josh? Where are you?"

He hurried toward her. "Here. Can I borrow that? My light just gave out." He reached for hers and whispered, "Stick close."

He shone the light in the direction he'd heard the sound. A mouse scuffled across the floor and disappeared under a box.

Bec stifled a squeal.

Better a mouse than a prowler. Josh turned the light back to the yellow trail and traced it to a shelf where her grandfather had stored fertilizers.

"What is that?" Bec asked, staying close on his heels.

"You said a real-estate agent was here today? Winslow?"

"Yeah, he was already here when I got home."

"So he could have been here for some time?" Long enough to pour sulfur down her well.

"I guess. Why?"

"This is sulfur. My guess is he poured it down your well to help persuade you to sell. Leaky roofs and contaminated water supplies are just the kinds of things that prompt city folk to pack up and sell."

"You think Winslow contaminated my water?"

Something shifted behind them.

"Watch out!" Josh pushed Bec to the ground and threw himself over her. Tins and gardening tools rained down on his back. He shielded her head with his arms. Then a crushing weight slammed into him, and his breath escaped in a huff.

He shoved off the tipped-over shelves, and a puff of chemical-smelling dust bit at his throat.

Bec coughed.

Josh scrambled for the light he'd dropped. "You okay?"

"Yeah, I think so."

The barn door slammed against the wall, followed by a blast of wind and rain.

"I've got to go after him." Josh quickly lifted Bec out of the debris and set her on her feet.

"My crutches."

He flashed the light back to the mess on the floor and pulled out her crutches. "You going to be okay here?"

"Yes, go!"

Josh skirted around her and dashed for the door, pausing at the threshold to give her enough light to get out safely.

"Go back to the house," he shouted over the wind and swept the beam over the yard. Visibility was near zero in the teeming rain.

Bec secured the barn door, then peered into the darkness with him, water sluicing down her yellow slicker onto bare calves. "Did you see which way he went?"

"No." Thunder rumbled. "We're never going to find him in this." Josh strained to listen for the sound of running feet, an engine, something. He tipped the light toward Bec's face. "Did you lock the house?"

Her eyes widened. "No."

He jogged across the lawn with Bec not far behind, swinging her crutches double time.

Sarah pulled open the door. "You two okay?"

"You see which way the guy went?" Josh motioned Bec inside ahead of him.

"What guy? I didn't see anyone." Sarah stepped back as Bec shrugged off her dripping coat.

No way could the guy have gotten inside without leaving a wet trail. "Okay, stay inside and lock the door." Josh turned his light back to the yard.

Lightning fractured the blackness, followed by a bone-shuddering crack.

The guy could have holed up anywhere, but he had to have gotten here somehow. Josh grabbed his keys from his pocket and jumped into his truck. He sped to the farm lane, where he'd spotted Smith's car the night Bec had first arrived, but there were no fresh tracks. He angled his truck so the headlights pointed in the direction Smith had claimed to have followed the guy he'd seen run out of her barn. Still nothing.

He circled the block. But in the pelting rain, he could scarcely see the road in front of his headlights, let alone a car that might be tucked in behind the hedgerow. He drove back to Bec's.

The instant his foot hit the porch step, she opened the door. She'd changed into dry clothes, but her hair hung in wet ropes around her face. "You didn't find him?"

"No."

"Do you think it was Winslow? Why would he come back?"

Josh checked the phone line coming into the house, then stepped inside. "I don't know. Where's Sarah?"

"She went up to bed."

Josh frowned. How could she sleep?

Bec handed him a towel. "Do you think this could have been Henry?"

"I doubt it. He's a P.I. investigating the jewelry theft. Claims he wasn't in the barn the night you were attacked."

"A P.I., for real? Do you believe him?"

"I don't know." He'd half expected to find the guy parked in Bec's driveway when he got back. "The P.I. part is true. The good news is he doesn't suspect your grandparents of involvement in the jewelry heist."

"Well, that's a relief anyway."

Josh glanced at the stairs. "Except it means we have no idea who we just chased out of the barn."

"Are you going to call this in?"

He imagined the captain's response if he did and shook his head. "No, I'm going to pay Winslow a visit. If he's just getting home, looking like something the dog dragged in, then I'll nail him." Josh picked up Bec's phone.

Still dead.

Had to be from the storm. The line wasn't cut.

He hated to leave her not knowing where this guy had disappeared to, but if Winslow was their culprit, this might be their only chance to prove it. "I won't be long. Keep the doors locked and your cell phone handy." He ruffled the dog's ears. "And keep Bruiser nearby."

* * *

The shopkeeper gave Becki an apologetic look and pulled the help-wanted sign from the store window. "Sorry, the position's been filled."

She trudged out the door to Serenity's main street. What was this? Some kind of conspiracy?

She'd never been turned away by so many employers in her life, let alone in one day. So much for job hunting taking her mind off last night's prowler.

Josh's sister had warned her the job market was tight. But to be turned down for a waitressing job?

Becki shoved her crutches into the backseat of the car. Yeah, who wanted a waitress on crutches? She should have listened to Josh and waited a few more days. But now she had a roof repair to pay for. If she didn't find a job, she'd never be able to afford the upkeep and taxes on the house, let alone eat!

Do unto others as you would have them do unto you.

Becki cringed at the memory of the morning's verse in the devotional booklet Gran kept next to the coffeepot. Was God trying to tell her that she needed to sell the house?

Is that why she couldn't find a job?

Becki slumped into the driver's seat. Most of the time she managed to ignore all the little God things Gran had scattered about the house. She'd always considered herself a believer, even if she didn't go to church as regularly as she had during the summers spent with Gran and Gramps. But had she ever really owned a faith of her own?

If she had, she wouldn't have ranted about God letting the squirrel build a nest in the chimney. Would she? Or hesitate to help Sarah?

Except, as much as seeing Sarah's bruises had broken her heart, she couldn't see how giving her sister more money would resolve anything. Inviting Sarah to move in with her might, but she still hadn't been able to voice that particular offer. Not after waking to find Sarah bringing a cup of coffee out to Josh's truck this morning.

Apparently, after he'd returned from Winslow's last night, he'd camped out in Gran and Gramps's driveway to keep watch.

Becki couldn't believe that she'd fallen asleep before he returned. Except that she'd felt safe, knowing he was out there hunting down her prowler.

The hair on the back of her neck prickled.

Her gaze shot to the street, the sidewalk, the shop windows. Josh had warned her to stay alert. Was it merely the power of suggestion that prompted the eerie sensation she was being watched?

Her gaze slammed to a halt at the barbershop window. Or, more precisely, at Bart Winslow standing at the window, looking her way.

His dad had been snug and dry in his home when Josh had paid him an unexpected visit last night. But Bart hadn't.

Josh had found him at the bar on the edge of town, drenched from the rain. Problem was, the puddles under Bart's feet didn't prove he'd been at her place. Half the people in the bar had been soaked from their dash for the door from the parking lot.

Bart disappeared from the barbershop window and an instant later emerged on the street.

Becki stuffed her key in the ignition, but she couldn't bring herself to turn it. Without evidence, Josh hadn't been able to do anything more than warn Bart to stay away from her. She didn't feel like sticking around to see if Bart intended to oblige, but she sure wasn't going to give him the satisfaction of thinking he'd scared her.

He paused outside the barbershop door, his gaze zeroed in on her windshield, although she wasn't sure he could see her with the sun glaring off the glass. His lips curved into a slow smile. Then he winked and headed in the opposite direction.

Okay. That was creepy.

Part of her wanted to swerve in front of him and tell him that he and his father should forget about ever getting their hands on her property. But the remote possibility he was just—well—a creep kept her foot off the gas.

She needed to get home anyway, make sure her sister wasn't getting into mischief. Sarah had offered to pick up groceries and cook them a nice supper, but maybe that glimpse of Sarah's bruises last night had made Becki too trusting.

When she pulled into the driveway a few minutes later, Bruiser and Tripod ran from the backyard together to greet her. "Well, hello. Glad to see you've made friends with the neighbor." Becki gave them each a thorough rub, noting that Josh's truck was back in his own driveway, then headed inside through the front door.

The aroma of fresh-baked chocolate-chip cookies greeted her.

"Mmm, those smell delicious." Becki tossed her purse on the bench in the entrance and clomped on her crutches to the kitchen. "If you're going to bake, you can stay as long as you want!"

The kitchen was empty.

Sarah's laughter floated through the back screen, followed by hammering.

Becki grabbed a couple of cookies and joined her sister on the porch. "What's so funny?"

Sarah motioned toward the roof. "Something Josh said."

Becki gaped up at Josh, shirtless, on her roof. "What are you doing?" She instantly clapped her mouth shut, hoping that didn't come out sounding as insanely jealous as it had sounded to her own ears. Her sister was a married woman, and…and…Becki wasn't interested in Josh that way. Not anymore. Not really. She shouldn't be.

"Patching your roof."

"But…shouldn't you be at work?"

"It's my day off. Other than that court appearance I had this morning."

"Oh."

He hammered on another shingle, then climbed down the ladder and pulled on his shirt. "All done." He plucked the second chocolate-chip cookie from her hand and took a giant bite.

"Hey!"

"This wasn't for me?" His expression turned all innocent, but she didn't miss the grin tugging the corner of his lips.

Becki rolled her eyes. "What kind of man steals from a cripple?"

Laughter danced in his eyes as he popped the other half into his mouth. "A hungry one."

Sarah scurried to the door. "I'll bring out a plate with more."

Becki squinted up at the roof. "I really appreciate your taking care of that for me." She sank into a chair. "I don't think I could have afforded to hire a roofer."

"No job prospects yet?"

"Not a one."

Sarah flounced back outside carrying a tall glass of lemonade and a plate loaded with cookies. "I thought you'd appreciate a cool drink, too."

Becki squirmed in her seat. Since when had Sarah turned into Suzie Homemaker?

Sarah took the chair opposite Becki and motioned Josh toward the one beside her.

Josh rested his hip on the arm and leaned toward Becki. "What if I told you that I got a gig for you?"

"A gig?"

"A freelance writing gig. If the editor likes what you produce, he'll give you more assignments."

"Are you serious? With what publication? On what topic?"

"For the region's tourism magazine, on touring in an antique car. The editor wants you to go on an upcoming weekend tour and write about the experience."

"That's awesome. Oh, wow. I can't believe it." Her heart felt like a helium balloon floating skyward. Light and carefree, soaring above the clouds. Then suddenly it popped. "But how will I get the car there? I've never towed a trailer."

"That's where I come in."

"Really? You'll come with me?"

"Yeah. It's kind of a condition of the assignment." Josh caught Becki's hand. "You okay with that?"

"Abso—" Meeting his gaze, Becki's answer stalled in her drying throat.

The phone rang, but Sarah popped from her seat and said she'd get it almost before Becki registered the sound. The instant Sarah disappeared inside, Becki yanked her hand from Josh's hold. "What are you doing? My sister's going to think we're dating or something."

"Yeah, that was the idea."

Her jaw dropped. He wanted to make Sarah jealous?

Josh hooked his finger beneath her chin and nudged it closed. "I figured your sister would be more likely to stop pressuring you to sell if she saw you had someone on your side." He slanted a glance toward the door. "All afternoon, she's prattled on over how concerned she is about you living out here alone."

Becki's goodwill toward her sister evaporated at the realization that she'd been working Josh to support her cause.

"For the record, I'm still uneasy about your being here, too, but I wasn't about to lend support to *her* agenda."

"Thanks." Becki tucked her hands under her legs. "What about this writing gig? Please tell me that wasn't an act."

His grin whisked away her worry. "Nope, that's a go. I guess I'll need to pick up the trailer." He glanced at his watch. "Anne's coming for supper, but I have time to do that first."

Josh stood. Then he suddenly caught Becki's hand again. "Your sister's coming back."

Becki tried to ignore the butterflies that fluttered through her middle as his arm came around her waist, bringing her face within inches of his. He was enjoying this game way too much.

"Do you want to come with me?" he said huskily.

Her gaze dropped to his lips, which spread into an I-know-what-you're-thinking smile. Mortified, she placed her palm on his chest to push him away, only his heart was beating as crazily as hers. Not an act?

He covered her hand with his. "Maybe it's better if you stay here. I'll be back soon."

TEN

Josh backed the box trailer up to Bec's barn as the girls made their way from the house.

The breeze teased Bec's honey-brown curls, and reflexively, his fingers curled.

Every time he saw her, he had this crazy compulsion to tug her into his arms. A compulsion that was getting more difficult to chalk up to wanting to get Mrs. O'Reilly off his case or to putting Bec's sister in her place.

She filled his thoughts when they were apart. And—Lord, help him—he liked that she needed him. When she'd tumbled into his arms during last night's storm, he'd been ready to do whatever he could to soothe away her tears.

It had taken every ounce of his self-control not to flatten Bart when he'd found him last night. He might not have been able to prove it, but he'd been positive Bart had just come from Bec's barn, no doubt scheming more ways to *persuade* Bec to sell if the sulfur in the well didn't do the trick.

Josh had to thank the guy for one thing, though. He'd sure proved Bec's determination to stay in the old place. If the freelance job Josh lined up for her panned out, maybe he could start believing that she'd stick around, work through her grief.

Sarah circled the trailer, looking stunned. "I had no idea Gramps had gotten so serious about touring."

Bec handed Josh the keys he'd asked her to find. "Maybe this wasn't such a good idea," she murmured.

He reassuringly curved his arm around her waist. "I think that's curiosity, not dollar signs, you see in her eyes." He thumbed through the keys. "These aren't for the trailer door."

"Those were all I could find. Are you sure Pete didn't have them?"

"No reason why he should. He only worked on the outside."

Sarah twisted the knob on the side door. "You're in luck. It isn't locked."

"It's not?" Josh skirted past Bec. "Your grandfather always kept it locked. He kept all his tools inside."

Sarah opened the door and gasped.

Josh's gut clenched. The Graws' touring costumes and duster jackets were strewn across the floor. The drawers of the cabinet their grandfather had built to hold his tools and clothing accessories were ripped out and overturned. Hatboxes were stomped. And the walls were pitted with dents.

Bec appeared at the doorway and let out a pained sound.

"I'm sorry, Bec. I should have checked on the trailer days ago."

"This isn't your fault," she said so softly he barely heard her over the roar in his ears.

Sarah lifted a dress from the floor and fitted it back onto the hanger.

Josh clasped her elbow. "Leave it. I'll want to take photos and dust for prints before anything's moved."

Nodding, she handed him the hanger. Without a word, she jumped down from the trailer and headed inside, while Bec remained frozen in the doorway.

Josh pulled out his cell phone and called in Hunter to help with evidence collection. The captain could hardly protest this time. Phone call made, he rejoined Bec. "I'm afraid this changes everything."

"What do you mean?"

"Winslow may have poured sulfur down your well, but I don't think he did this. This doesn't look like the work of someone trying to scare you into selling."

"Who, then?"

"Whoever did this was looking for something. And it wasn't the Cadillac."

The color drained from Bec's face. "The jewelry?"

"Possibly."

She stared through the open door at the destruction. "That P.I. knew about the trailer. He asked about Gran's costumes, acted like he'd be interested in buying them. I told him they were stored in the trailer."

"Did you tell him where it was?"

"No, but...now that I think about it, after he heard that I didn't have them he turned down my invitation to come in for coffee. You'd think he would have jumped at the chance to ask more questions."

"Yeah, unless he hoped to pocket the jewelry himself." Josh shook his head. "I can just imagine what my captain will say if I throw that theory at him. But whoever's behind this is clearly losing his patience. And that makes him dangerous."

Bec's fingers curled into fists. "Clobbering me with a two-by-four seemed plenty dangerous to me!" She had fire in her eyes, but the quiver in her lip pierced his heart.

Josh drew her into his arms. "We'll get this guy."

Hunter pulled into the driveway in a patrol car and joined them, carrying a camera and an evidence kit. "What do we have?"

Bec slipped from Josh's arms and readjusted her grip on her crutches. "I'll wait inside with Sarah."

Hunter poked Josh with his elbow. "So the scuttlebutt is true?"

"What?" Josh snapped his gaze from watching Bec's retreating back. "There's another lead on the case?"

Hunter laughed. "I'm talking about you and Bec."

"What about us?"

"That you finally found someone you're willing to hang up your bachelorhood for."

"Don't be ridiculous. She's my neighbor and in trouble. I'm just trying to catch a bad guy here."

Hunter shrugged. "If you say so."

"It is so."

"That's not how it looked a minute ago."

"That's an act for her sister's benefit," Josh said automatically, even though Sarah had been the last person on his mind. He raked his fingers through his hair. Hunter *would* have to arrive just as he was giving Bec a reassuring hug. He'd acted on instinct, but Hunter didn't need to know that.

Hunter looked over his shoulder and every which way. "What sister would that be?"

Josh jerked his hand toward the house. "She just went inside."

Hunter cocked his head and studied Josh with one squinty eye. "You missed your calling."

"What calling?" Josh shot back, losing his patience.

"Undercover, man. Any cop who can act that good should be working undercover."

Josh motioned to the trailer. "Just get in there and take your pictures."

Hunter whistled as he stepped in view of the devastation. "You might want to reconsider that car tour you'd planned." He jumped the foot and a half onto the trailer and snapped a picture. As he focused the camera on one of the dents in the wall, he added, "From the looks of it, this guy's ready to blow a gasket."

"Yeah, Bec's not going to be happy when I break the news that we can't go."

"Then again..." Hunter opened the trailer's back doors, letting in more light. "If we're looking for a jewel thief after all, you might pick up on a suspect if you hit the car tour."

"I can't put Bec at risk."

Hunter photographed the large wrench the guy had likely used to smash the walls. "I have the weekend off. I could go along, if you like. Watch your back."

"A single guy in the backseat?" Josh commandeered the evidence kit. "That'd be a sure tip-off."

"I could drive an old car, too. My uncle has a Model T I could borrow. Your sister's a good sport. She'd probably agree to come along and ride shotgun."

"I'm not bringing my sister into this." Josh brushed powder across the wrench handle, cringing at the thought of what else this creep might do with such a weapon.

"She was tough enough to work the E.R. in Detroit for three years. Do you really think this guy's going to scare her?"

"Probably not. And that's enough reason to not ask her to come along."

"Ask who to come along where?" Anne's voice came from behind him. "Whoa, what happened?"

"Someone got into the trailer," Josh said, but Hunter lowered his camera and opted to answer her first question instead.

"I suggested you and I could join Josh and Bec on a double date."

"Really?" Anne's face lit up.

"It's not a date," Josh growled. "He's talking about the car tour I told you about."

"I'd love to come."

Josh ground his teeth until his jaw hurt. "We can't go now. It's too dangerous."

Anne motioned toward the destruction. "Any more dangerous than staying here?"

"Why do you think? Everything in the trailer was strewn all over. The walls were bashed."

Becki's hand froze on the porch door handle. Who was her sister talking to?

Becki edged toward the open kitchen window. Normally, eavesdropping was not her modus operandi, but when some jerk destroyed Gran's special clothes and her sister sounded as if she knew who, normal no longer applied.

"I'm sorry." Sarah's voice suddenly sounded as small as a five-year-old's. "I didn't mean to…"

At the sudden silence, Becki inched forward another step and peeked inside.

Sarah cowered on the floor, her back pressed to the cupboard, her knees tight to her chest, trembling. "No, I'm sorry. I wouldn't. You know I wouldn't. I don't know what came over me. I…I was just upset over seeing—"

If Becki wasn't seeing her sister with her own eyes, she'd never believe it. Sarah had never kowtowed to anyone. Who had this kind of power over—

The question balled in Becki's throat as her gaze dropped to Sarah's bruises. When Josh had wrapped Becki in his arms and promised her they'd get this guy, she'd scarcely been able to believe that she was in any real danger. Had Sarah ever felt that safe in her husband's embrace?

"Of course," Sarah said into the phone. "I love you, too."

Becki jerked back from the window as Sarah rose and hung up the phone.

What's going on? What do I do?

Love your enemy.

The thought boomed through Becki's mind.

Was that what her sister had become? An enemy?

The patio door slid open, and Becki sprang to attention. "Hi."

Sarah glanced from Becki to the open window and flinched.

"You okay?" Becki asked gently.

"Sure, why wouldn't I be?"

"Who were you talking to?"

"No one." She gathered the empty glasses and plate from the patio table. "Probably chattering to myself. I do that a lot." Sarah turned back toward the door with the dirty dishes.

Becki touched her arm. "Talk to me."

"I don't know what you mean."

"Sarah, you're my big sister and I love you."

Sarah gulped. "I love you, too." She rushed inside.

By the time Becki maneuvered through the door after her, Sarah was squirting dish soap into the sink. She didn't look Becki's way. "You should get off that foot. It's never going to get better if you don't rest it."

Becki sank into a kitchen chair. Her ankle throbbed worse than the day she'd twisted it, but she wasn't about to admit it. "Do you think Rowan tore apart the trailer?"

"*No!* Of course not."

"Look, Sarah, I'm not going to lie to you, even if you're bent on lying to me. I heard you on the phone. It sure sounded to me as if you thought whoever was on the other end had ransacked the trailer."

Sarah set a dish in the drying rack and answered without turning. "I called Rowan because I was upset. I was just telling him what happened. He didn't like hearing me so upset. That's all."

"Is Rowan having trouble at work?"

"No, they love him at the law firm. In another year they'll probably make him a partner."

"If he's doing so well, why does he care about scraping a few more dollars out of our grandparents' estate? He has to know that with what you've already received, even if I got top price for this house, you wouldn't get much more than another fifty thousand. He must make that in less than half a year."

Sarah dropped the dish she'd been washing and sudsy water splashed over the lip of the counter. She grabbed a tea towel and sopped it up, then turned her panicked gaze to Becki. "You can't tell him you're thinking of selling."

"I'm *not* thinking of selling!"

Sarah's shoulders sagged with what seemed like relief, which was bizarre, because she'd spent the last how many weeks begging Becki to sell?

Becki squinted at her, and suddenly the puzzle pieces dropped into place. "You want more money, but you don't want him to know?"

Sarah balled up the tea towel and tossed it onto the counter. "I want to leave him, okay?" She stormed out of the kitchen.

"Sar-aaahhh," Becki called after her. "Come back here. Talk to me." She reached for her crutches, knocked one gliding across the floor and hopped to the doorway instead.

Sarah sank into Gran's favorite armchair, her elbows on her knees, her hands over her face. "I can't believe I said that. You can't ever tell him."

With Sarah's sleeves pushed up to her elbows, allowing a full view of her yellowing bruises, Becki didn't need to ask why. "Move in with me. You can live here." Peace washed over her the instant she said the words. That sense of family, of being with someone she could count on no matter what, that was what she'd been yearning for all along. What Gran and Gramps had always surrounded them with. "I know you never used to like living in the country. But Serenity might grow on you."

She shook her head. "I can't. This would be the first place he'd look for me."

"So you tell him you're through putting up with his abuse. If he refuses to get counseling and act like a civilized human being, demand a divorce. I don't care how good a lawyer he is. You'll still be entitled to half his estate and to alimony."

Sarah lifted her head and looked at Becki as if she'd just dropped off the turnip truck. "It's not that easy. Rowan doesn't believe in divorce."

"Neither do you. But, Sarah, your vows didn't say anything about being his personal punching bag."

"He's under a lot of pressure at work. I shouldn't have brought up the credit card being denied."

"Don't you dare justify what he did to you."

Sarah burrowed her face against the armrest. A moment later she turned her head and met Becki's gaze. "I can smell Gran's perfume."

"On the armrests." Becki loved to sit there to read for that very reason. "Gran always dabbed it on her wrists."

"I wish she was here. She always knew what was best."

"Stay with me, Sarah."

She shook her head. "I can't. I won't put you in any more danger."

ELEVEN

Josh waited for his sister to drive away, and then, as promised, he headed over to Bec's to discuss what they'd do next. She stood at the rail of her back porch, watching the sunset, and didn't seem to hear him approach.

He quickened his steps, trying not to notice how beautiful she looked against the crimson sky. He'd let his empathy get the better of him earlier when he'd wrapped her in his arms. Or maybe on some level, he'd feared the vandalized trailer would be the final straw to drive her away.

She shivered.

He shrugged out of his flannel jacket and dropped it over her shoulders, resisting the urge to let his hands linger. "Better?" he said as he lifted her hair free of the collar and inhaled its fresh scent.

She burrowed into the jacket with a grateful smile. "Much. Thank you."

He forced himself to put another foot between them. "Would you rather talk inside?"

Bec glanced at Sarah through the patio door. She sat at the kitchen table working on a crossword puzzle. "No, out here is better."

Bec seemed to want to say more, but she turned back to the sinking sun and curled her fingers around the porch rail.

Josh rested his forearms on the rail next to her. "This was your gran's favorite time of day."

"I remember."

"She once told me that sunsets reminded her how God works behind the scenes in ways we can't always see. The colors are there in the light the whole time, but we don't see the amazing picture He's painting until the light is fractured."

"Kind of ironic that happens just before night, huh?"

Maybe it was the coming darkness or maybe the despair in Bec's voice, but Josh couldn't help himself. He enfolded her in his arms and pressed a kiss to the top of her head. "We'll get this guy, Bec. I promise. We didn't pull any prints, but Hunter's running a more extensive background check on that P.I., and we'll canvas the neighbors around Pete's Garage." His heart ached at the way she melted against him, as if she'd grown too weary of fighting. "I'm afraid we should bow out of this car tour, though," he murmured.

She sprang from his arms. "What? We can't. It's the only job offer I have."

"Your safety is more important."

She bristled at his brusque tone.

He softened his voice. "Bec, we have no idea who this guy is or why he's targeted you. If he's connected to the jewelry theft and hears you're on the tour, there's no telling what he might try."

Bec shook her head. "He's not."

"What do you mean? Do you know who ransacked the trailer?"

Her gaze slanted to the kitchen door. "I think it was my brother-in-law."

"The attorney? For a bigger cut of the inheritance? It's one thing to launch a legal challenge, but a guy like that isn't going to risk a criminal charge and tanking his career for a few extra grand."

"You're forgetting that I'm the only person that stands between him and the *entire* estate."

A kick of fear swiped Josh's breath. Would her brother-in-law murder her for the money?

Hadn't the notion crossed his own mind last night?

Her brother-in-law had the strongest motive of anyone. But… "If Sarah's husband wanted you dead, he would have taken you out that first night in the barn."

"Maybe that wasn't him. You think Bart Winslow poured sulfur down the well. Maybe he left the note, too. Or…" Bec clutched his arm, her eyes widening. "Maybe Rowan staged the attacks to make it look like I had a stalker. He had to know that if he didn't divert suspicion and I turned up dead, he and Sarah would be the prime suspects."

Josh's heart thundered. As unlikely as the theory sounded, it was just the kind of elaborate scheme a crooked lawyer might pull. "Do you think Sarah knows? If you're right, I mean."

"She suspects." Bec wrapped her arms around her waist. "I think I overheard her call him on it. I doubt he's stupid enough to try anything more now."

Josh turned to the door. "I want to talk to her."

"No, please." Bec grabbed his arm. "She'll deny it. She's embarrassed and ashamed. But she's my sister. I trust her."

"What if you're wrong?"

"I'm not." Her voice was firm, but even in the deepening shadows, Josh didn't miss how her gaze blanked, betraying no hint of what she was thinking.

"What aren't you telling me?"

Her fingers tightened around his arm. "I need you to trust me. Okay?"

His mind flashed to the last woman he'd trusted, then the string of them, right back to his mother. Bec had no idea what she was asking of him. "I need evidence to put this guy away."

"I don't have any. Believe me, I'd give it to you if I did."

He let out a sigh, not sure what to believe. He'd run a background check on Sarah's husband the same time he'd run Neil's. Nothing had come up to suggest Rowan would turn psycho on his sister-in-law.

Josh squinted at the darkening fields. "I don't like you and Sarah being alone in the house."

"We're not alone. We have Bruiser." Bec handed him back his jacket. "And as for the car tour, I know that I'll be perfectly safe with you."

There was no use arguing with her. Truth be told, her sincerity swept any words from his lips. So he simply nodded, knowing somewhere down the road she'd change her mind about him, and he'd be right back in the middle of heartache.

Becki nestled in the passenger seat of her sister's BMW and laughed at Sarah's imitation of the heroine in the movie they'd just watched. After a week with no more incidents, she finally felt able to relax. Maybe Sarah had brought Rowan to his senses or Josh had spooked the guy off—whoever the guy was. Becki was just glad that the trouble seemed to be past. Of course, it helped that her ankle finally felt better, too. "This feels like old times. Remember when Gran and Gramps used to take us out on Tuesday nights to watch the latest movie?"

Sarah chuckled. "The movies were never exactly the latest. I think Serenity brought films in only days before they released on DVD."

"I never cared. I just loved going out like a family." Becki turned in her seat to face her sister. "I wish you'd reconsider moving in with me. Maybe if you separate from Rowan for a while it will smarten him up, make him figure out what he stands to lose."

Sarah threw her a wry look. "Let's not spoil the evening by talking about Rowan, okay?"

Becki released a sigh. The more she'd tried to coax her sister into facing her marital problems, the more Sarah had closed off. She'd even denied that Rowan had ever hit her or that her cryptic *I don't want to put you in any more danger* had been a reference to what he might do to Becki if she interfered.

Becki turned her attention to the side window and the black night beyond. She couldn't understand her sister's loyalty to the man. Becki would rather live the rest of her life alone than stay married to a man who hurt her.

Her thoughts skittered to Josh. How *not* alone he'd made her feel since moving here. How safe she felt in his arms. How that would change if he ever up and married.

Piercing blue headlights skirted across the side mirror.

Becki squinted against the blinding light. "Learn to drive," she muttered under her breath. Nothing irked her more than people who drove on her bumper, especially with their high beams glaring into her mirrors.

At least they'd be turning off on the next road.

Sarah made the left. But a moment later, their tailgater did, too.

Becki spun in her seat to look out the rear window. The car had an unusual shape. Nothing like those of any of her neighbors.

A hundred yards from their driveway, Sarah started to slow.

"Keep going. Don't turn in," Becki ordered.

"What? Why?" Sarah shot back. Thankfully she pressed the gas anyway.

"There's someone following us, and the last thing I want is to give him the chance to corner us in our own driveway." She whipped out her phone and punched Josh's name.

He answered on the first ring. "Hey, Bec, what's up?"

"Someone's following my sister's car."

His tone instantly turned urgent. "Where are you?"

"We just passed the house. It could be nothing, but he's riding our bumper and I don't recognize the car."

"I'm on my way. Turn right at Spiece Road. If you see lights on in the Spieces' house, pull in there. If not, keep driving. I'll—"

"Josh? Josh, are you there?" Becki glanced at her screen. "Lost reception."

"Is he coming?" Sarah demanded.

"Yes. He said to turn right on Spiece."

Sarah's attention jerked to the rearview mirror. "Oh, no!"

Becki whipped around as blinding headlights swept the car. An instant later, the car pulled alongside theirs.

"He's trying to push us off the road!" Sarah screamed, fighting to hold the wheel steady.

The car kept pace with theirs, edging dangerously close.

Sarah eased off the gas.

Becki grabbed the dash. "Don't stop!"

The guy in the other car motioned for them to pull over.

Sarah gasped. Touched the brake.

Becki braced for impact. "Don't stop, Sarah!"

Her cell phone rang.

Becki snapped it on. "Josh, he's trying to push us off the road."

"I'm on Spiece. Where are you?"

"Still on Elm." Becki glanced over her shoulder. "We missed the turn. Hurry!" To Sarah she yelled, "Why are you slowing down?"

"It's Rowan," Sarah whispered.

Her husband whipped his car ahead of theirs and touched his brakes.

"Go around him," Becki ordered, terrified he'd kill them both.

"I can't." Sarah jerked the car to a stop.

Ahead of them, Rowan burst from his car.

Becki reached across her sister and slammed the door-lock button.

"What are you doing?" Sarah hit the button again. "That'll only make him more angry."

Becki slapped the button a second time. "Better out there than in here. Josh will be here any minute."

"Oh, that'll go over real well—bringing a cop to the scene." Sarah unlocked the door and pushed it open before Becki could stop her.

Rowan yanked the door wide. "Did you think I wouldn't find out that you lied to me?"

Sarah shrank against the side of the car. "What are you talking about? I told you I was coming to help my sister."

Becki burst out the passenger side. "Don't you dare touch her!"

"This is none of your business," Rowan seethed.

"Stay out of this, Becki, please," Sarah pleaded.

"I won't." Becki rounded the front of the car, wishing she still had her crutches to take a swing at him if he laid a hand on Sarah.

Josh's patrol car swung onto the road and barreled toward them.

"What lies has she told you, huh?" Rowan ranted. "She told me she was coming here to find out what was taking so long for the inheritance to come through."

"But—" Becki stopped. He wasn't after her share? She shot her sister a questioning look.

"Yeah." Rowan leaned his face into Sarah's and sneered. "Why do you think my pretty little wife let me think she didn't have it?"

"Freeze!" Josh crouched behind his car door, gun—no Taser—aimed at Rowan.

The red-and-blue lights strobed over Rowan's face, turning his sneer into something uglier. "You called the cops on me?"

"Hands in the air," Josh ordered, stepping from behind his door and taking a cautious step forward.

Becki's breath caught at the sight of a red dot painted on Rowan's chest.

He looked down at his chest, and his hands instantly shot into the air. "This is a misunderstanding, Officer. My wife didn't realize I was looking for her and got scared when I drove up behind her."

Josh drew closer. "Step away, Sarah."

"You know this cop?" Rowan hissed, his hands still in the air, but looking as if he wanted to give her a good shake.

"From childhood." Sarah's voice came out small and scared.

"Sarah, step away," Josh repeated more forcefully.

She inhaled, regaining a couple of inches, and after an apologetic glance in Becki's direction, she turned toward Josh. "I'm sorry. Becki called you for nothing, Officer Rayne. Like my husband said, it was a misunderstanding."

Josh's gaze narrowed. "Did he lay a hand on you?"

"No! What do you think I am?" Rowan took a deep breath and exhaled slowly. "Look, Officer…Rayne, was it? I've done nothing wrong. I'm a lawyer and am fully aware of my rights."

"Well, I suggest you use your right to remain silent." Now that Sarah had stepped out of Rowan's reach, Josh holstered his gun. "Sarah?"

"What?" Sarah's gaze skittered from Rowan to Becki before returning to Josh. "No, he didn't touch me. This was nothing."

Becki started toward her sister. "Sarah, those bruises weren't nothing. Maybe—"

"It was nothing," Sarah repeated more adamantly. "My husband was understandably worried about me." She offered Josh an apologetic smile. "I'm sorry we troubled you."

Josh's concerned gaze shifted to Becki. "Did you see anything different?"

Becki almost wished Rowan had grabbed Sarah's arm.

Josh was obviously looking for a reason to haul him in. But she couldn't lie.

They'd clearly overreacted when they thought he wanted to push them off the road. Not to mention it'd be his word against theirs, and she suspected Sarah would side with him.

After hearing that Rowan didn't know the estate had already been settled, Becki wasn't so sure he was even her prowler.

She shook her head. "He didn't touch her."

"On the phone you said he tried to push you off the road."

"I just pulled alongside them," Rowan said, lowering his hands. "So she could see it was me." He turned to Sarah and brought her hand to his lips. "Babe, I'm sorry I scared you. You know I love you."

Josh returned his attention to Becki. "Is that the way it looked to you?"

She let out a sigh. "Yes."

"It's probably best I head home," Sarah said.

"No, you can't. I mean, I'm sure Rowan won't mind your staying longer."

"Your ankle's better. You don't need me any longer. I'll drop you off and pick up my suitcase."

Becki gaped at her sister. How could she agree to go home with this man, knowing how furious he was over his discovery about the inheritance?

Becki threw Josh a wordless plea. *Can't you do something?*

TWELVE

Josh opened the car door as Bec hurried from the house. She'd captured her hair into a ponytail, and that, along with her ruffled skirt and tie-dyed shirt, made her look as if they should be driving a 1970s Chevy instead of a 1913 Cadillac.

"Any word on Rowan?" she asked.

Last night it'd been all Josh could do to get her to calm down long enough to relay everything she knew about her brother-in-law. When she'd poured out her suspicions about the bruises she'd seen on her sister's face and arms, Josh had felt sick. If only she'd told him sooner, he might have come up with a legitimate reason to detain the jerk.

"There was one domestic call to their address eighteen months ago. A neighbor complained of shouting. No charges were filed."

"Nothing since?"

"Not on record, but my friend promised to dig deeper. In the meantime…" He motioned for her to climb in. "What do you say you try to relax and enjoy the ride?"

He'd hoped a drive to the old quarry would distract her from fretting over her sister all day.

"Sorry. I've just been so worried."

"Yeah." He knew the feeling. He'd pulled a couple of favors just to get the day off so he could watch over her. Taking the car for a test run before the tour had been the perfect excuse to get her out of the house. He slid in beside her and showed her again how to start the car.

She pulled on the choke and pushed the ignition button, but nothing happened.

"Try pushing the button at the base of the steering column. The flood bowl might have dried out." It hadn't been sitting long enough for that to be likely. The car had run fine last week.

She tried again. Still nothing. "We got gas?"

"Oops." He'd been so preoccupied, he'd forgotten to check. He grabbed the gasoline can from the corner of the barn, thinking he might've picked a more picturesque spot to run out of gas.

"Why, Josh…" Bec leaned out the car window and fluttered those impossibly long eyelashes of hers. "If I'd known you just wanted to go parking, I'd have worn something more becoming."

He chuckled, but that didn't stop the heat from climbing to his face. He unscrewed the gas cap. "We've got plenty of gas." He topped it up anyway.

"I guess you'll have to crank her."

He groaned. Last time he'd done that, the thing had backfired and ripped the crank out of his hand, almost breaking his wrist. He set the gas can aside and gave the crank three and a half quick turns, being careful to keep his thumb off to the side just in case. "Try it now."

The engine sputtered to life.

"We're good." She laughed as he climbed back in. "It always sounds like a sewing machine to me." Struggling to master the clutch, she clunked it into a stall.

"Try again," he urged.

This time she turned smoothly onto the road and flashed him a victorious smile that gave him a kick of pleasure.

As Bec experimented with changing gears on the hilly gravel roads, he sat back and enjoyed the view. Her sun-kissed cheeks glowed in the morning light, and her mouth quirked in the cutest way whenever she had to step on the clutch.

She stopped at a stop sign on a steep hill, and when she managed to start again, he gave her an approving elbow nudge. "You're a natural."

"I know why Sarah's been after me to sell," Bec said, her mind apparently on a different road than his altogether. "I think she wants to disappear."

He instantly sobered. "You think she's *that* scared of her husband?"

"She practically said as much when I invited her to stay with me."

"Do you really think he'd risk his career to maintain control over her?"

"I think he'd risk everything. Why else keep secret that she already had her inheritance payout?"

Josh focused on the winding road and braced himself for where this conversation was headed. Bec was being utterly unselfish, but he didn't want her to sell the house and leave Serenity.

Bec shot him an apologetic glance with those gorgeous brown eyes, and hard as he tried to withstand the impact, his heart ached. He'd miss her more than he wanted to admit.

"I've decided I need to sell the car."

He blinked. "The car?"

"I'm sorry. I know how much you love it, but I just don't feel right holding on to something so valuable when I could use the money to help my sister."

"You're a pretty great sister."

Her cheeks were tinged pink. "You're not mad?"

"How could I be mad?" His heart practically soared. He'd rather have Bec around than an old car any day.

A few strands of hair broke free of her ponytail and whipped across her cheek. She tipped back her head and laughed.

Josh reached across the seat and tucked the strands behind her ear.

The laughter in her eyes turned to panic as the car barreled down the hill.

"The brakes! I have no brakes." Bec white-knuckled the steering wheel.

"Pull the emergency."

"Where is it?" Her gaze darted from the winding road to the center of the car, where she'd expect it if the driver's seat were on the left.

"By the door!" Josh reached across her lap and pulled the lever.

The car didn't slow.

Bec veered around a corner. "What do I do? It's picking up speed."

"It's okay. Gear down."

She played the clutch and shifted to a lower gear.

The engine whined higher, but the car slowed only a fraction.

Trees blurred by.

"Take it down another gear. Ride it out until we reach the bottom of the hill. You're doing great."

Except with two hairpin turns before the road leveled, great might not cut it.

What idiot designed a car with a blocked driver's door?

"We're going too fast!" she screamed. "I can't make the curve!"

"Yes, you can." With no seat belts, if she didn't make it, they'd be airborne whether they wanted to be or not. "Lean into the curve."

Halfway around the bend, the outside tires caught loose gravel. He grabbed the steering wheel and cranked hard to the left.

The car kept going straight. Straight to the ravine.

Trees raced toward them.

Josh kicked open the passenger door, clamped his arm around Bec's waist and hauled her across the seat. Her screams reverberated through his chest.

"Jump!" He sprang through the opening, dragging her with him. *Oh, God, please don't let her die.*

Becki opened her eyes and slowly lifted her head. Her fingers squished through muddy leaves, and for a terrifying instant, she imagined she was feeling Josh's bloodied body. She pushed to her knees. "Josh?"

A groan rose from a few yards away.

She scrabbled toward the sound, her breath frozen in her lungs.

His face was scraped and bruised and ghostly pale.

Her heart fisted into her ribs. "Oh, God," she whispered, unable to finish her desperate prayer as she clasped his arms. "Josh?"

Glassy eyes met hers, looked at her as if he'd been given a precious gift. "Bec," he whispered, real tears in his eyes.

She brought his hand to her cheek. "You saved us."

"You're…okay?" The question came out pained, breathless.

"Yes."

He slid his fingers through her hair, looking as if his entire world had nearly careened off that cliff with the car. Then he pulled her to his chest and held tight. "Thank God."

She wasn't sure how long she stayed wrapped in his arms, listening to his pounding heart begin to slow, feeling his warmth melt away the terror. But it was too long.

So long that she let herself start to imagine what it might be like to be wrapped in his protective arms every night. So long that she let herself imagine that she could have a relationship like Gran's, not like her mom's or her sister's. So long that she let herself forget that Josh didn't think of her that way.

She eased out of his embrace. "We need to call for help."

His hand trailed down her arm as if he didn't want to let her go. Then he reached for his hip. "I must have lost my phone when we jumped."

She scanned the ground, but neither his phone nor her purse were anywhere in sight. She eased sideways down the embankment toward her mangled car.

The roof had been sheered. The front end bashed. The driver's side crushed.

"Gramps's car," she whispered.

Josh drew to her side. "I'm sorry, Bec. I should have checked—"

"No, this isn't your fault."

"Someone's been terrorizing you from the day you got here. I should have been more diligent."

She froze in her tracks. "You think Rowan—" She cupped her hand over her mouth, unable to form the words. He could have killed her. "I've got to call Sarah. Warn her to get away from him."

Josh caught her arm. "Wait. We don't know if *anyone* is behind this yet."

Surging from his grasp, she scanned every which way for her purse. If there was the slightest chance Rowan had done this, Sarah needed to be warned.

"There." Josh pointed to a filthy mound wedged like a squashed melon beneath the driver's side of the car.

She gulped. That could have been her head.

Josh pressed his shoulder into the upturned car and heaved.

She yanked the purse free and fished out her phone.

Josh stayed her hand before she could connect. "You'll only incite her husband more if you start making allegations. If he's behind it, we don't want to alert him until we have proof." He pried the phone from her hand. "Let me call Hunter." A moment later he spoke into the phone. "It's Josh. The brakes went on the Cadillac...No, we're fine. But can you send a tow truck to Deadman's Hill?"

Becki took back the phone the instant Josh disconnected. "Why didn't you tell him your suspicions?"

"Trust me. It's better if we have proof first." Josh examined the underside of the car, which sat perpendicular to the rocky ground.

"See anything?"

"The cotter pin is missing. But I'll need more proof than that."

Becki turned the phone over and over in her hand. She hated waiting, not knowing, not being able to do anything. "She wants to leave him anyway. If she doesn't, who knows how badly he might hurt her the next time he loses his temper? And now I can't even help by selling the car."

Josh's hands shook as they touched the mangled metal. "I'll make out a police report. The insurance company will pay you something."

"But…" Oh, why didn't she pay more attention to all the paperwork the lawyer had given her? "I didn't contact the insurance company after Gramps died. What if they canceled the policy?" She walked around the upturned car. "There's no glove box. Where—"

"Careful." Clasping her shoulders, Josh pulled her away from the wreckage. He reached into a pocket on the door and produced the insurance slip. "Why don't you call them while we're waiting?"

He went back to examining the car's underside as she explained the situation to the insurance company. The rep grilled her with a gazillion questions, and even after she answered them all, he couldn't give her an answer.

She gave the car a swift kick.

"Whoa." Josh braced his hand on the car as if she'd kicked hard enough to topple it. "What'd they say?"

"They have to investigate, but it doesn't sound hopeful. They kept asking me why I didn't notify them when I took possession." She kicked the car again, because it was either that or burst into tears, and she did *not* want to cry on Josh's shoulder. He might have held on to her after the crash as if there was no tomorrow, but—she gave the car another hard kick—there wouldn't be any tomorrows. Not when it looked as if the only way to help her sister now was to sell the house.

Josh caught her from behind in a bear hug and yanked her away from the car. "It's okay. Everything will work out."

"It's not okay. It's never going to be okay. They're dead."

THIRTEEN

Josh turned Bec away from her grandfather's mangled car and tucked her head against his shoulder. Bits of grass and twigs fluttered from her hair, over his hands, inflaming the shame burning in his chest.

"I'm so sorry," he whispered. More sorry than she could ever know.

"I don't know what to do." Her tears dampened his shirt. "Sarah needs my help, but I don't want to give up the house. It's all I have left of them." Bec lifted her head and swiped at her eyes. "Why couldn't she have married you?"

He stiffened. *Sarah?*

"You would never have hit her," Bec mumbled against his shirt

His arms tightened around her. His gaze drifted to the wreckage, a glaring reminder of how utterly he'd failed her. "No," he whispered. "A wife should be cherished."

"Josh? Bec?" Hunter shouted from the crest of the ravine.

Josh eased Bec out of his arms. "Down here."

Hunter and a guy in blue coveralls, with Ted's Towing embroidered on the chest pocket, picked their way down the embankment. Hunter gave the scene a sweeping glance, his expression grim. "Are you sure you two are all right?"

Josh rubbed the shoulder he'd bruised taking the brunt of the fall to shield Bec from injury. But the shoulder didn't hurt half as much as the punch to the gut that came from Bec pairing him with her sister.

"I can call an ambulance."

"We're fine." Bec swiped at her damp cheeks. "I just want to get home and talk to my sister."

Josh winced. He needed to figure out what really happened before she said anything to Sarah.

The tow-truck driver circled the car and made a face. "Gonna take a while to haul this puppy out of here. I'll have to call in help to get it up that cliff."

Hunter took out his notepad.

Josh pointed to the rods. "The cotter pin that links these is missing."

"You think this was another attack?"

"Yeah. A cotter pin doesn't just slip out."

"You'd be surprised," the tow-truck driver said. "If it wasn't seated right, these rough roads could shake it loose, easy."

Some of the fear left Bec's eyes.

As much as he'd like to believe the theory might be true, Josh shook his head. "I don't think so. The emergency brake was tampered with, too."

The tow-truck driver scrutinized the cables. "Nothing wrong with the emergency brake. But it would've been useless on that steep incline."

"Sounds to me like we're looking at an accident," Hunter said.

Josh let out a pent-up breath. *Or the guy wanted it to look like an accident.*

Hunter filled out the police report the insurance company would require. "I guess you and Bec will have to join me and Anne in my uncle's Model T for the car tour now."

"Until I'm convinced this wasn't sabotage, the last place I want to take Bec is the car tour."

"Then I'll go on my own." Bec hiked up her purse strap,

fire in her eyes. "I have to write that article. I won't let him win."

Hunter tapped his pen on the notepad. "She's got a point."

"Are you nuts? Even if this wasn't sabotage, I knew she was a target and I didn't catch this. I can't risk—"

"Blaming yourself for this is as ridiculous as blaming yourself for not checking the Graws' chimney for squirrels' nests."

Josh couldn't draw a breath into his drying throat. *Please tell me you didn't just say that.*

Bec's strangled gasp confirmed the worst. She gaped at him. "You *saw* squirrels go into the chimney?" The question came out as a whisper, but there was no masking the utter betrayal that coated her words.

"No. I—" Josh cut off the explanation. Nothing could bring back her grandparents. No excuse could absolve him of responsibility.

He'd never registered her grandfather's bright red cheeks—the trademark sign that carbon monoxide was replacing oxygen in his blood.

Hunter looked as if he wanted to crawl into a hole.

Josh would've been happy to dig it for him, too. Not because he didn't deserve her derision. Because she needed protection more than ever, and now she'd want nothing to do with him.

Bec backed farther and farther away from him until she came up against a tree, her arms wrapped around her waist.

Josh swallowed, but he couldn't dislodge the wad of regret blocking his throat. He'd been to countless accident scenes. Held victims as they died. He'd even had to break the news to their loved ones. But not a single case had haunted him like the Graws' deaths.

Nightmares still woke him. If he managed to sleep at all.

"About the car..." Hunter mercifully interjected. "If it was sabotaged like you think, maybe keeping Bec away from the tour was what the guy wanted."

Josh shook his head. Strained to wrap his mind around Hunter's detour.

"Think about it. The first day she got here, the note in her mailbox said she didn't belong. Sounds like he doesn't want her in the house. And if she doesn't write the article, she won't get the job."

Bec straightened. "And if I don't get the job—" her voice pitched higher "—I can't afford to stay in the house."

Josh ground his fists deep into his pockets and stared at the wreckage—another connection to her grandparents that she'd lost. If she couldn't keep the house, she'd be devastated.

Following the crash, his only thought had been to thank God he hadn't lost her. Except he couldn't lose something he never had.

"C'mon." Hunter flipped closed his notepad. "I'll give you both a lift home. You can hash this out there and let me know what you decide about the tour."

"You're forgetting that besides Anne and us, her sister is the only one who knew about the writing job."

Bec's face paled. "Sarah wouldn't have done this."

Josh didn't know what to think anymore. He needed to put his emotions aside and look at the facts. Figure out who did this and why. And whether he *or she* would try again.

The next morning, frantic barking yanked Becki from her sleep. Bruiser clawed at the bedroom window, looking as if he might sail through any second.

Becki sprang to her feet and grabbed his collar. "Easy, boy." Staying low so she couldn't be seen, she peered outside.

At the sight of the barn's open bay door, her breath caught. They'd had the tow-truck driver unload the wrecked car inside, but who would want it now?

She reached for her cell phone to call Josh.

Her stomach tightened. Josh was the last person she wanted

to face right now. She snuck another peek out the window. Okay, maybe the second last.

Tripod scampered out of the barn.

Tripod? Becki let Bruiser's collar go. If Tripod was outside, then Josh had to be up. She squinted at the clock: 5:30 a.m. Didn't the man ever sleep?

No, he'd probably stood guard all night despite her protests. *And he calls me stubborn.*

Bruiser whimpered at her bedroom door.

"Yeah, okay. I'm coming." She quickly threw on a pair of jeans and a T-shirt and opened the door.

Bruiser soared down the stairs, skidded to the kitchen door and started barking again.

"Hold your horses. I need my shoes."

Bruiser snatched up one of her sneakers and pranced in a feverish circle as Becki dropped onto a kitchen chair. The dog deposited the shoe at her feet.

Becki swiped the slobber off the laces. "Thanks."

Ten seconds later, she pushed open the door, and Bruiser took off for the barn, barking loud enough to wake the town three miles away. He raced straight for Tripod at full speed, and they tumbled in a ball of yipping fur. A prowler didn't stand a chance.

Becki wavered at the kitchen door. Josh must be going over the car again—one more thing he felt he owed her for. She didn't even blame him for her grandparents' deaths. It was just hard to face him, knowing how differently things might've turned out. She'd never thought that she'd rather be considered a needy stray, but it beat being his penance.

She drew in a deep breath and ambled to the barn. She couldn't avoid him forever.

"You don't have to do this," she said loud enough for Josh to hear…wherever he'd disappeared to.

His head popped out from beneath the car. "Sorry, I didn't mean to wake you."

"Should've thought of that before you opened the big door and set off my dog siren."

He rolled out from under the car and onto his feet. "At least one of us is doing our job." He snatched up a rag and wiped the grease from his hands.

So she was a job. Well, that was better than penance. "I thought you gave up trying to prove the brakes were sabotaged."

"Wanted to see what it would take to salvage her for you."

"But the insurance adjuster said she'd be a write-off even if they honor Gramps's policy."

"Doesn't mean she can't be fixed. Just means they think it'd cost more to repair than it's worth."

"Well, if they pay me, the money's going to Sarah. I already told you that."

He tossed the rag onto his tool chest and picked up a ratchet. "My labor's free."

For the first time since she'd moved there, she felt as though Josh was the one who needed her, instead of the other way around. Needed to know she didn't blame him for not preventing her grandparents' deaths. "You don't owe me anything," she whispered.

He bent over the engine and ratcheted a part. "I like to tinker. Remember?"

She wedged open the crumpled rear door and slid onto the backseat, the way she used to when Josh and Gramps would tinker together. She scratched at the chipped paint on the door frame, and Gramps's deep baritone whispered through her mind. *God wouldn't settle for just slapping on a coat of paint to fix that, would He? He wants to change us from the inside out. Not just change what people see on the outside, because—*

"God's in the business of restoration," she said aloud. She sensed Josh studying her, but she focused on the chipped paint. "How do you do it?"

"What's that?"

"Keep believing when…God doesn't seem to care."

"I focus on the things that show me He does."

"My grandparents are dead. My sister's husband is beating her. I almost got killed—"

"*We* didn't get killed." He put down his ratchet, leaned over the door. "Your grandparents passed peacefully in their sleep to a new life. You've reconnected with your sister, grown to understand her better. You have a home in the country like you've always wanted."

Bruiser raced into the barn and planted his giant paws on the door beside Josh.

Josh ruffled his fur. "And we can't forget your fiercely protective dog."

"Or my even more protective big *brother.*" She winced. She hadn't meant to emphasize the last word. Fortunately, Josh didn't seem to notice.

"See how easy it is to notice God's blessings when you start looking?" A dimple dented his cheek, but his smile didn't reach his eyes.

"My grandparents were good at that. They never doubted God's love even when my dad rejected them. I want to know God the way they did."

He covered her fingers, which had been chipping away at the paint. "You can."

"Josh," she said softly, "I don't blame you for what happened." Their eyes met, and…he looked so tormented, she wished… She looked away, dug her fingers into the gap between the seat cushion and the back of the seat.

"Hey, I think I've found something." She wiggled her fingers, straining to catch hold of whatever it was. "Maybe it's what the thief was after." She twisted onto her knees. "My fingers aren't long enough."

"Here, let me have a go." Josh climbed in beside her, and the air filled with the homey scents of clean soap and pine.

His hair, still damp from his morning shower, grazed her arm as he leaned over to reach between the cushions.

Trying to savor the moment despite herself, she withdrew her hand to give him more room. "It's right in the middle there."

"It feels like paper. Got it." He pulled a small notebook free from the cushion.

"Oh, that's mine!" Nostalgia bubbled up inside her at the sight of the long-forgotten book. "That's what I used to write my stories in." She reached for it, but he moved it out of her reach.

"Your stories, huh?" He flipped through the pages.

She tried to grab it from him, but he stretched his arm so she'd have to climb over him if she wanted it.

"Let's read one. See if they're as good as I remember."

She lowered her hands. "Really? You thought they were good?"

"Sure." He brought the book to his lap and thumbed through a few pages before suddenly stopping. "This one sounds like it'll be interesting. 'When I grow up,'" he read.

Becki gasped and snatched the book from his hand. Now she remembered how the notebook got between the cushions…and why.

"C'mon, Bec. It'll be fun. You always had a great imagination."

Oh, she had imagination all right.

He reached around behind her and recaptured the notebook.

"No!" She flailed her arms after it. "Please give it back," she said firmly. "I don't want you to read it."

His grin fell. "I thought you'd get a kick out of hearing the stories again. You were always reading them to your Gramps and me when we worked on the car."

"I know, but—" She grabbed back the notebook. There was a good reason she'd stuffed this particular notebook deep between the seat cushions the instant Gramps and Josh had returned from their trip to the scrap yard all those years ago.

"Is it a diary or something?" he asked. "About your parents?"

"No, nothing like that."

"Then what's the big deal?"

She shimmied across the seat and climbed out. "It just is. Okay?" It was bad enough she'd started to imagine that he'd finally noticed her after all these years when he'd only had a guilty conscience.

He scooted out after her. "Now you've just made me all the more curious."

"Well, you know what they say about curiosity."

"Yeah, it's a good trait."

"No, it killed the cat!"

He leaned back against the car and casually crossed one leg over the other. "'When I grow up, I'm going to marry Joshua Rayne,'" he recited as if he had X-ray vision and could read the pages through her hand.

"You saw that?"

He grinned wickedly.

"Argh!" She turned away and buried her face in her hands.

His strong, muscular arms encircled her. His scent enveloped her. "Hey," he whispered, his breath lifting the hair from her neck. "Why are you embarrassed? I'm flattered. I want to read the rest. Find out what happens."

She leaned back, and her head collided with the solid wall of his chest. "I was twelve."

"I'll keep that in mind." Amusement flickered in his voice.

But what was the point in making a big deal about it if he'd already seen the worst?

"Fine." She slapped the notebook against his chest. "Read to your heart's content."

She climbed back into the car and continued digging between the cushions for real clues.

"'We'll live in a big farmhouse like Gran and Gramps,'" Josh read, resting his forearms on the edge of the car window. "I like that." He grinned.

She ignored him.

"'We'll have lots of animals, because we'll take in all the injured ones God brings our way,'" he read on. As he turned the page, he added, "You and I rescued our share of animals over the years, didn't we?"

Becki chuckled. Josh had never stopped—rescuing animals or damsels in distress.

"'Josh wants to be a farmer. I like that, because I don't want him to be away from home all the time like Daddy is.'" Josh's voice quieted, and she wondered if it was from the reminder of his lost dream or the mention of her father. "'We'll have lots of kids. At least two of each. Jeffrey, Josh Junior, Jessica and Jenny.'"

His meadow-green eyes captured hers. "You named our kids," he whispered.

"I was twelve."

"I love those names."

Her heart skipped a beat. "You do?"

He closed the notebook. "Except if we have a Josh Junior, we'd need to have a little Becki, too."

"But of course." She played along. It was just like old times, sitting around the campfire as kids, weaving far-fetched stories.

"We already have a three-legged dog, a bird with a broken wing and Bruiser."

She laughed. "Yup, a steady supply of needy animals won't be a problem with your reputation."

His grin snagged her breath. He grazed his fingers along her cheek, the color in his eyes darkening, his expression growing intense.

He was *serious!*

His gaze dropped to her lips, and he slowly stroked his thumb across them.

She held her breath, certain she must be dreaming. Certain any second she'd wake up to Bruiser licking her face.

He cradled her face in his hands, his fingers curling beneath her hair, and looked at her as if he couldn't believe she was real. Had she been wrong? It wasn't guilt that had him being so protective…so near so often?

He traced her lips with whisper-soft butterfly kisses. No, definitely not guilt.

She slipped her arms around his waist and kissed him back. He tasted of sweet meadows and babbling streams and an abandon that took her breath away.

FOURTEEN

Josh waited for Hunter to drive his uncle's Model T into the box trailer, then helped secure the holding straps. "You're sure your uncle won't mind my taking the car for tonight's reception?"

"What's to mind? You're just transporting it. Anne and I will meet you there tomorrow." Hunter double-checked the straps. "How'd Bec talk you into going on the tour anyway?"

"Let's just say she can be very persuasive." Josh strained to contain the smile tugging at his lips. He could still taste her kisses, feel the warmth of her arms encircling him. He hadn't wanted to let her go. Ever. He sure wasn't about to let her go on the tour without him.

Not that Hunter needed to know any of that.

Hunter laughed. "Man, you've got it bad."

"What are you talking about?"

Hunter slapped him on the back. "She's already got you henpecked."

Josh shrugged off Hunter's hand. "I happen to admire her determination not to give in to this creep's tactics. *And* I want her to nail this writing job as much as she does."

"So she can afford to stick around, huh?"

This time Josh didn't bother to rein in his smile. "You've got to admit she's better than any neighbor you've ever had."

Hunter hopped down from the box trailer. "Why don't you just marry her?"

"What?" Josh stubbed his toe and grasped at the car's fender. He missed and stumbled off the end of the trailer.

Hunter roared with laughter. "Oh, man, you should see your face."

Josh turned his attention to shoving away the ramp. It wasn't as if he hadn't entertained the idea of marrying Bec. Entertained it a hundred times over since reading her journal. He'd even imagined what their children would look like with Bec's adorable curls.

"I knew from the minute you called to borrow the cameras that she'd gotten to you."

Josh slammed shut the trailer's back doors. "Yeah, right."

"I'm serious. After the shooting, all the guys noticed that she wasn't *just* a neighbor."

"I was concerned about her safety."

"And that Winslow might ask her out. And that she might not find a job here and would have to sell." Hunter leaned against the trailer, his expression smug. "Marrying her would solve all your worries."

"That's crazy. She's only been here a couple of weeks." And already he couldn't imagine his life without her.

"Sure, but you've known her all her life. Didn't you say Graw told you he proposed to her grandmother after only three weeks? Look how well that turned out."

True. And from what Bec had written in her journal, they'd always wanted the same things. If all this trouble didn't scare her into running back to the city, maybe… He shook the crazy notion from his head. "It's too soon. She hasn't even found a job here yet."

"Wouldn't matter if you married her."

"Don't go blurting that to her this weekend. Your mouth has already gotten me into enough trouble." Then again… Josh tossed his truck keys in the air and caught them.

Maybe this time Hunter would be doing him a favor. "I've got to run. She'll be waiting for me."

"Give me a sec to grab a wrap," Becki called out the front door as Josh drove into her driveway, his truck window open. Her insides bubbled at his lopsided smile and the anticipation of feeling that smile on her lips again. The way he looked at her warmed her clear down to her toes.

She lifted the long skirt of her gown and turned back to the foyer. What was she after?

Oh, yes, a wrap. Now, where did she see some?

She flipped up the lid on the bench where Gran had always kept a supply of winter hats and mitts. Her eyes lit on a silk scarf. Ooh, that would make a gorgeous wrap. She snatched it up, and an evening glove tumbled out. Something pinged across the tile.

Bending to take a look, she stopped short at the sight of a gold-and-ruby earring. She turned it between her fingers. The design was old, older than anything she'd ever seen in Gran's jewelry box. Old enough to be a museum piece.

Her stomach pinched. It couldn't be. She quickly searched the scarf. No other pieces were wrapped inside, not even the matching earring.

She breathed a relieved sigh. Gran must've worn the earring during one of the car rides and didn't realize it caught on her scarf. The match was probably sitting in Gran's jewelry box upstairs.

Becki studied the piece again, ignoring the churning in her stomach. Okay, she was 99 percent sure that she hadn't seen anything like this the last time she'd checked Gran's jewelry box, but that didn't mean the earring was a museum piece. A visitor who'd borrowed one of Gran's scarves for a ride could have lost the earring.

Becki set it on the hall table so she'd remember to look for its mate when she got back and, spotting a long white glove that had also tumbled from the scarf, scooped that up.

A necklace spilled out.

Her breath caught in her throat.

This couldn't be what it looked like. Becki slumped to the floor. Gran must've taken the necklace and earrings off while away and stored them in her gloves for safekeeping, then forgot about them.

Except…Becki held the glove by two of its fingers and gave it a shake.

Cuff links, a pair of earrings and a matching necklace and bracelet tumbled to the floor.

No! Becki lifted one of the black onyx cuff links. An *M* was monogrammed on it in tiny diamonds. *Montague.* The name blazed through her mind along with the image of this very piece—the image she'd seen in the newspaper article about the jewelry theft.

The sound of Josh's truck door slamming cut through the air.

Her heart hammered. She couldn't let Josh see these before she figured out what to do. She stuffed the cuff links back into the glove, then scrambled to scoop up the other items.

The front door burst open. "I grabbed your mail. Are you just about—"

Becki's gaze snapped to Josh, her fingers tightening around the fistful of stolen jewelry.

"Are those—"

She sprang to her feet and backed away from him. "I was going to tell you."

He slapped the mail onto the hall table and halved the distance between them. "Where did you find these?"

"This can't be what it looks like."

"Where did you find them?" he repeated.

She pointed mutely to the deacon's bench. Before she could

stammer out a word, he started pulling out hats and mitts and scarves.

"They were inside the evening glove."

"Where's the other glove?"

She scanned the pile he'd emptied from the bench, shook out the scarf. "I don't know. Gran usually kept the gloves with her costumes in the trailer or in the cedar chest in her room."

Josh commandeered the single glove and jewelry and motioned her to the kitchen. He laid the items out on the table. "Why would you hesitate a second to tell me you found these?" He sounded like a father scolding a six-year-old, but apparently the question was rhetorical, because without waiting for an answer, he pulled out his cell phone and scrolled through his contact list.

"We can't turn them in yet," she blurted.

"Why on earth not? Don't you realize what this means? Your attacker must have been after the jewelry all along and may be more desperate than ever to recover it." He put the phone to his ear. "We turn them in. The media reports they've been recovered, and he'll have no more reason to bother you."

"No." She snatched away his phone and hit the power button. "If we turn them in before we figure out how they got here, the police will blame Gran and Gramps for the robbery."

"Bec, I'm a police officer. I can't *not* turn them in!" He pried the phone from her fingers.

Okay, she was upset and, yeah, probably being unreasonable, but... "How can you let Gran's and Gramps's reputations be destroyed?"

Josh stroked his thumb across her knuckles. "I promise we'll figure out a way to clear their names. I'll ask the investigating officer to keep the source of the recovery quiet. Chances are no one around here would ever learn of your grandparents' connection anyway."

"They're not connected! See, even you're talking as if they stole them."

"Bec, you know I don't want to believe that, but how do you explain their being in the house?"

"Maybe the guy who broke in planted them."

Josh cocked an eyebrow. "*Planted* them?"

"Okay, that doesn't make sense, but he searched the car first, right? So he must've put them in there, and when he couldn't find them, he figured Gramps had taken them inside. Gramps probably found the scarf in one of the door pockets and figured Gran had just forgotten to bring it in."

"Sounds reasonable. I'll suggest as much to the investigating officer, and he'll look into it."

"No, he won't. He'll pin this on Gran and Gramps because it saves him work. It lets him close the case in a neat and tidy package." The twitch in Josh's jaw confirmed her fear. Budgets were stretched to the snapping point these days. If they could close a case, they would.

"I doubt the detective will keep quiet about the source, either." Becki twisted the necklace between her fingers. "The robbery made network news. The recovery will, too. They always sensationalize everything."

"We'll make sure the truth gets reported."

"When? Three weeks later when the news stations have moved on to the next major story? No one will hear that Gran and Gramps have been cleared of any wrongdoing unless we prove it before we turn in the jewelry."

Josh shook his head. "We can't hold on to stolen goods. I understand your fear, Bec, but it's illegal."

"I don't care!" Why did he have to be so…responsible?

"You could go to jail. Is that the kind of legacy you want for your grandparents?"

"Are you going to arrest me?"

"No, of course not."

"Then if I figure out who stole these before I turn them in, it won't matter what they do to me."

"You're being reckless. This is not some elaborate childhood scenario we've concocted around a campfire. These are real stolen goods. There's a real thief out there looking for them. You have no concept of the risk you'd be taking."

"I am not a child!"

He clasped her hands. "Your grandparents wouldn't want you to put your life at risk to clear their names."

The tenderness of his touch, the pleading in his eyes, clutched at her heart, but she couldn't let him change her mind. "I need to do this," she whispered. "Don't you see? They were the only people who ever accepted me just as I am."

His grip on her hands tightened, his expression pained. "Not the only ones, Bec."

She gave her head a violent shake and yanked her hands free. "You don't understand."

"I do. I want to clear their names as much as you, but I care more about keeping you safe."

She surged to her feet. "I am not some bird with a broken wing that you can lock away in a cage for my own good."

"That's not what I'm doing."

"Yes, it is. It's what people have done to me my whole life. I'm tired of everyone else deciding what's best for me. I'm doing this."

Josh caught her arm. "I can't let you."

She lifted her chin defiantly. "Can't or won't? Because I thought you were someone I could count on."

After a long pause, he shook his head. "Has anyone ever told you how obstinate you are?"

She quirked a half smile, certain the resignation in his voice meant he'd play this her way.

"It wasn't a compliment," he huffed.

"But you'll help me?"

"Yes, just not the way you're asking." He snatched a Baggie from the kitchen drawer and swept the jewelry into it.

"What are you doing?"

"Turning in the recovered property. I'm a police officer. That's what police officers do."

For a moment, she couldn't utter a word, just stared at him in disbelief. "If you do this, I'll never speak to you again."

"Real mature," Josh said, as if Bec were still the kid she was behaving like. She'd used the same I'll-never-speak-to-you-again line on him dozens of times, usually just before he tossed her into the swimming hole.

She planted her hands on her hips. "I mean it."

Yeah, she used to say that, too. He never should have argued with her this long. "I'll be back as soon as I can. Stay inside and keep the dog with you." He turned away and forced himself to open the door and keep walking. There was no reasoning with her when she got like this.

As he unhitched the trailer from the truck, he second-guessed his decision a dozen times. He climbed into the truck and slammed the door. He had no choice. Hopefully, by the time he returned, she'd be cooled down enough to keep the truck cab from overheating for their trip. Then they could discuss how they might go about clearing her grandparents of any suspicion.

Not the conversation he'd hoped to have during their drive this evening.

Her rant about being tired of everyone else deciding what was best for her roared through his mind as he sped off.

He had a bad feeling she wouldn't get over this as easily as being thrown into the swimming hole.

What was she supposed to do now?

From the living-room window, Becki frowned at the trail of dust still swirling from Josh's hasty departure. The man was downright infuriating.

She snatched up the mail he'd tossed onto the table. At the sight of the insurance company's return address on the top envelope, she sucked in a breath. Her hands shook as she slid a thumb under the flap. She unfolded the paper and her gaze stopped on the second word—*regret*.

"No!" She slumped onto the bottom step.

Bruiser rested his head in her lap and nosed her hand with an apologetic whine.

"It's okay, boy. You didn't do anything wrong. It's…" She crumpled the letter in her fist. "Why, Lord? I don't want the money for me. I want to help my sister."

Bruiser retreated to the doormat.

Becki stared up at the ceiling as if God might actually answer, but no answer came.

After a long while, she lifted the skirt of her gown and trudged upstairs. The last thing she felt like doing now was attending the evening reception. She hung the gown back in Gran's closet and pulled on jeans and a T-shirt.

Her cell phone jangled.

He changed his mind! She grabbed the phone. "I knew you wouldn't let Gran and Gramps down."

"What are you talking about?" her sister asked. She sounded as if she'd been crying.

"Sarah, what's wrong?"

Sarah sniffled. "I left him."

Clutching the phone to her ear, Becki dropped to a chair. "What happened?"

"It doesn't matter. I just needed to warn you."

"Warn me?" Becki's thoughts whirled to the gunshots, the car accident, the bruises on her sister's face. "Where are you? I'll come get you."

"No, your house will be the first place he'll look for me."

Her heart clenched at the tremor in Sarah's voice. "Do you have money?"

"Becki, I didn't call to ask for money. I'm sorry I ever asked you to sell the house. You shouldn't have to pay for my mistakes."

The regret in Sarah's voice stripped away the last of Becki's irritation with her. She'd misjudged her sister terribly. How had they drifted so far apart?

"Maybe one day, when it's safe," Sarah went on quietly, "I can come back."

"Come *now*. I can't bear to lose you, too." Becki swallowed a sob. She'd made such a mess of everything.

"I can't, Becki. I just can't. I have to get far away. Go somewhere that Rowan wouldn't think to look for me. I'm sorry."

The real-estate agent's card stared up at Becki from where she'd tossed it next to the phone all those days ago. She picked it up, set it down, picked it up again. "I'll sell the house," she heard herself whisper into the phone.

"What? No, you can't do that. You love that house. And what about Josh?"

Crushing Winslow's card in her hand, Becki stifled a sob.

"What's wrong? What did he do?"

"He betrayed me." Becki pressed her bunched hand to her mouth. She hadn't meant to say that. Sarah had enough problems without getting into hers.

"How?" Disbelief laced Sarah's voice.

"Oh, Sarah." The pressure building in Becki's chest erupted like a volcano. "There was a jewelry theft. At the last tour Gran and Gramps were on."

"Gran and Gramps would never be involved in anything like that."

Becki stuffed Winslow's card into her pocket and swiped at the tears leaking from her eyes. "We found the jewelry here in the house, in one of Gran's gloves in the hall bench."

Sarah gasped. "A glove?" she said faintly.

"I begged Josh to help me find the real thief before he turned in the jewelry. But he refused. Gran's and Gramps's reputations are ruined."

"The police think they stole the jewelry?" Sarah's voice cracked.

"That's how it looks! Josh said he'd tell the police they didn't, but... Oh, Sarah, I know he's a cop, and he has to do the right thing, but..."

"Why couldn't *you* come first for once?" Sarah finished softly.

Yes. Becki traced the image of her father standing with Gran and Gramps in a photo sitting nearby. "Maybe we could've lured the thief to reveal himself at the car tour somehow. Now I don't know how we'll ever prove their innocence."

"I have an idea."

Becki's heart leaped. "What?"

"You'll see! This tour starts with a reception at the Grand Hotel, right?"

"Yes." Becki tipped aside the curtain on the window facing Josh's house. "We were about to leave for it when I found the jewelry."

"Okay, I'll meet you at the hotel."

"But what about Rowan?"

"He'll never think to look for me there."

"Josh isn't back yet." Becki surged to her feet. After his "real mature" quip, she wasn't all that anxious to ask for his help, but she'd eat crow a hundred times over if it would help clear their grandparents' names.

"All the better. Come alone."

"I can't tow that monstrous trailer!"

"Don't bother with it. You can ride along with other drivers. It'll be all the better for your article. Give you a chance to experience a bunch of different cars and gather the owners' stories."

Her article! She'd been so concerned about clearing her grandparents' names she'd completely forgotten about the freelance opportunity. Not that she'd need to win over the editor once she sold the house. Her heart hitched at that thought.

Outside, gravel crunched and the purr of a car engine went silent.

She jogged down the stairs. "He's back."

"Is he coming to the house?"

A head bobbed past the living-room window.

Becki sucked in a breath. "It's not Josh. It's Neil."

"That's perfect. Ask him to drive you. Didn't you say he was a car fanatic, always going to car-club shows?"

"Yeah, 1960s sports cars, not horseless carriages."

"Still, you know he'd jump at the chance to spend the weekend with you."

The doorbell rang, and Bruiser went ballistic.

Her heart thudded against her rib cage. "I don't want to give him the wrong idea," she whispered frantically even though Neil couldn't possibly hear her.

"Leaving your car in the driveway will throw Rowan off my trail. Besides, might be good for Josh to see you out with someone else. Make him jealous."

Becki's jaw dropped. *That* would be immature. "All I care about is protecting our grandparents' reputations."

"Then head out now with Neil, or alone. It's getting late. If you don't hurry, we'll miss the reception."

The doorbell rang again.

"I'll see you in two hours." Sarah clicked off.

"Quiet," Becki ordered Bruiser and grabbed his collar before pulling open the door.

"Whoa." Neil backed up a step.

"It's okay." She released Bruiser's collar and patted his behind. "Go on out, boy."

Neil stepped inside without waiting for an invitation.

Becki pasted on a smile. "Neil, what a surprise." She hitched her thumb over her shoulder. "I'm afraid I was heading out. I have to meet my sister for a car-tour reception."

His gaze traveled up from her ratty jeans to her wrinkled T-shirt and stopped on her face, probably splotchy from crying. "Like that?"

"I was about to change." She backed up a step, feeling

oddly uneasy. She wrote it off to Sarah's jealousy comment about Josh and drew in a deep breath. After the way Josh had ignored her pleas and walked out on her, she shouldn't be the one feeling guilty. "Was there something you wanted?"

Neil took in the foyer, front room and eating area in one sweeping glance. "Doesn't look like you've changed the place much."

"No, I like it the way it is."

"Was the dog your grandparents'?"

"No, he's new."

Neil nodded, looking as discomfited by their stilted conversation as she felt. His gaze drifted around the room again, then settled on the hall table. "Wow, this is an impressive piece." He picked up an earring—the stolen earring she'd found in the scarf!

In all the rigmarole, she'd forgotten to add it to the rest. Funny that its match hadn't turned up, either.

"Your grandmother's?" Neil asked, holding it out.

"Yes," Becki said automatically, then bit her lip at how easily the lie had slipped past.

Neil rolled the earring between his fingers. "Looks like it could be worth a bit. You shouldn't leave it lying around."

"You're right." She scooped it from his hand. "I'll put it back now." She took another step backward toward the base of the stairs, even though she knew she couldn't go up until she got rid of Neil.

"Were you heading to the reception alone?"

"Uh…" The mantel clock dinged the hour. *Hurry, hurry,* her thoughts whispered. How long would Josh be? Dare she wait? Did she even want to?

"Yes, actually, I am going alone. Would—" The invitation lodged in her throat.

"Would you like an escort?" he offered with an old-fashioned bow.

She recalled how Gran would giggle when Gramps greeted

her that way, and she wished she could feel that giddiness, too. Becki had to admit she didn't relish the idea of a two-hour drive alone in the encroaching darkness. "If you'd like to join me," she heard herself respond.

"What are friends for?"

His expression was friendly, undemanding, but the uneasy feeling crept down her spine again. She shook it off. It was just the way the evening had been going that made her so unrealistic. "Give me a few minutes to get dressed."

Neil glanced at his dark dress slacks and crisp white shirt. "Am I okay?"

"You'll be fine." She hurried up the stairs to her grandparents' bedroom, where she dropped the earring into Gran's jewelry box and then went to the closet.

Her fingers glanced over the emerald satin gown that Josh had wanted her to wear. She lifted out the red one next to it and frowned at the low neckline.

"That one's very nice."

Becki startled at Neil's voice behind her. She clutched the dress to her chest and whirled toward the door. "What are you doing up here?"

"Thought you might need some help." He leaned casually against the door frame. "Those earrings would look stunning with that dress. Did your Gran have a matching necklace?"

"Uh, I'm not sure." She should have known the earring would pique Neil's curiosity. He prided himself on his expensive tastes, a trait that had taken her far too long to notice.

"Let's look." He strode toward the dresser.

"What? No. There's no time." She shooed him out. "You need to let me get dressed or we'll be late." She'd forgotten about his habit of making himself right at home, whether invited or not. Josh would never do that.

She locked the door behind him before peeling off her shirt and jeans. Winslow's business card tumbled from the pocket. *Do you care more about your sister than a house?* it taunted.

I do. If she wanted to help her sister, she needed to make the call.

Before she could change her mind, she dialed Winslow's number and gave him the go-ahead to list the house. Josh would be furious that she'd asked Winslow of all people, but if she put off the decision until she could find someone better, she'd talk herself out of it. Or…Josh might. She dressed quickly, then wavered at the bedroom door.

She couldn't just leave without telling Josh. What if he'd still planned to take her on the tour despite their fight?

Part of her—the part that could never stay mad at him—wished she had the courage to call and ask. But it was too late now. She jotted a quick note to tape to his door. She'd call his sister once they were on their way.

By the time Becki descended the stairs, Neil was checking out Gran's antique tea trolley in the living room. She pulled on a pair of long, white evening gloves she'd found in Gran's room. "I'm ready."

Neil's gaze widened, and he let out a low whistle. "You look stunning."

"Thank you, kind sir."

"Didn't find a necklace to go with the dress?"

Her hand splayed over her bare throat. "No. It's okay without, isn't it?"

"Exquisite."

Her face warmed. He could be very charming when he wanted to be. So why did his flattery make her feel so edgy tonight?

She shrugged off the sensation. Between finding the jewelry and fighting with Josh, not to mention learning Sarah had left her husband and deciding to put the house up for sale, anyone would be edgy.

He lifted the wrap she'd draped over her arm and dropped it on her shoulders. "This is a beautiful place. I can see now why you're so fond of it." He tapped the ornate paneled wood beneath the stairs. "Any trapdoors or secret passages like you see in the old movies?" he asked conspiratorially.

"Not that I know of." She opened the front door and let the dog in.

Neil took the hint.

Outside, Becki breathed a sigh of relief that Josh still wasn't home. She sent Neil over to tape the note to Josh's door while she called Sarah's cell phone to let her know they were on their way.

An automated message said, "The number you are trying to reach is no longer in service."

Returning to the car, Neil caught her arm. "What's wrong? You look like you've seen a ghost."

"I don't know. We need to hurry."

FIFTEEN

Only one thing could've made Josh feel worse than Bec feeling as if she couldn't count on him. Winslow was hammering it into her front lawn.

The man gave the for-sale sign one last whack and then scuttled back to his motorbike as Josh pulled into the driveway.

Josh rammed his truck into Park. He got that she was mad at him. Got it loud and clear. But mad enough to leave?

She loved this place. This place. Not him. He shoved the thought away.

He strode past her car and pounded on the back door.

Bruiser slammed his paws into the door with a howl, then sat back on his haunches and wagged his tail, tongue lolling.

"C'mon, open up. We're neighbors, Bec. You can't not talk to me forever."

Josh crossed his arms and watched for movement through the window. Figured she'd pick today to actually stick to her no-talking promise.

He shouldn't have walked out the way he did. When two more minutes passed and she still hadn't come to the door, he stalked to his house.

Deep down he'd known this day would come. With all the trouble she'd had, it was a wonder it hadn't come sooner. But for how desperate she'd been to clear her grandparents' names, the last thing he'd have expected her to blow off was tonight's reception.

If she still wanted to go on tomorrow's car tour, he supposed she'd let him know. In the meantime, he might as well take care of the animals so there'd be less for his pet-sitter to bother about. He stripped out of his old-fashioned getup, put on a pair of jeans, then got to work cleaning the birdcage. When he'd finished, he laid a fresh sheet of newspaper in the bottom and coaxed the lame bird back inside, wishing he could have won Bec's cooperation as readily.

"At least *you* understand that I just want to help you. Don't you?" he cooed to the tiny sparrow. "A woman with any sense would appreciate a guy who wants to protect her."

A chuckle rose behind him. *Anne.*

"They say talking to yourself is the first sign of senility."

Josh snapped the cage door shut. "What are you doing here?" He whistled for Tripod and lifted him into the laundry tub.

"Becki called and told me that Hunter and I were off the hook for the car tour."

Josh's heart jerked. So she was bailing on the tour, too. Not just tonight's reception. He schooled his expression and lathered the shampoo into the dog's fur. "I'm surprised she gave that up so easily."

"It wasn't your idea?" Anne sounded surprised.

Apparently Bec hadn't shared the rest of their discussion. "No. I was looking forward to the tour." Now that the jewelry had been recovered, he'd figured they could dig up evidence to clear her grandparents' names without the risk.

"But you were so worried she'd be in danger, I just assumed—"

"You assumed wrong." He focused on scrubbing the dog's coat, doing his best not to betray how irked he was that Bec didn't talk with him before canceling the tour. Never mind that she wasn't talking to him. He supposed now that she'd decided to hightail it back to the city, she didn't need the free-lance job. She was just like Mom and every other woman he'd ever tried to get close to.

"Stop it."

"Stop what?" He turned on the short hose he'd rigged to the tap and rinsed the dog's fur.

"Your infernal—" She waved her hand at the sink. "You always do this."

"Do what?"

"Fuss with your pets when you have people problems."

"I do not." Josh rubbed Tripod down with a towel and then lifted him to the floor. If Bec wanted to be childish and not speak to him, let her. He'd insisted the detective on the jewelry-theft case keep the Graws' name out of the paper. He was ready to turn over every rock to find the guy. What more did she want?

"How did you get Becki so mad at you?"

"Why should you care?"

Anne looked at him as if he'd just landed from another planet. "Because I've never seen you as happy as you've been these last couple weeks."

"You've got to be kidding. I've been a basket case worrying about Bec's stalker."

Anne's eyes sparkled. "And you've loved every minute of it."

Josh pushed past his sister and snatched up the kettle to fill. "That was an act for O'Reilly, remember? It didn't mean anything."

"Yeah right, that's why you've been doodling potential names for your future kids on the scratch pad by the phone."

"Get real." He glanced at the pad on the counter, then nudged it under the electricity bill. "I was trying out poten-tial bird names."

Anne caught the edge of the pad with her index finger and

drew it back into view. "Little Becki? Think she'd like having a bird named after her?"

"It was a joke." His thoughts drifted to the day he'd found her old journal, how right she'd felt in his arms, how his heart had soared to discover that she'd dreamed of them as a couple, a family.

"Right. Do you want to be single for the rest of your life?"

He set the kettle on the stove and snapped on the burner. "Is there a point to this conversation?"

"Do you know what Mom said after your high-school sweetheart ran off for the city?"

"Was that before or after Mom headed in the same direction?" Bitterness dripped from his words. He winced. He thought he'd gotten over his resentment. Anne was pushing all of his buttons today.

Anne lounged in a kitchen chair as if utterly oblivious to the thorn she'd twisted in his side. "She said it was for the best. That you didn't love the girl enough to marry her."

"How would she know?" And what did a high-school flame have to do with any of this? She was ancient history.

"Because I told Mom that the afternoon Charlotte left, you took apart that old Cadillac with Mr. Graw instead of chasing after her."

"She'd made her position clear. I wasn't enough to keep her in Serenity." Not for his mom, either, for that matter.

Anne leaned forward and pierced him with a hard stare. "When you really love someone, you'll fight for them no matter how far or fast they run."

Josh unhooked a couple of mugs, a spark of hope warming his heart. "Did Bec tell you that?"

"No. Mom did when Dad didn't chase after her and beg her to come home."

Josh pinched the bridge of his nose. But the pressure inside his head only escalated. "Maybe he was respecting her choice. Maybe he didn't want to make her feel worse for leaving. Maybe he figured if she really loved him she wouldn't have left in the first place."

"Are we talking about Dad or you?"

The kettle screamed.

He snapped off the heat. "Isn't there someone else you can irritate?"

"What's the worst thing that would have happened if you'd chased after your high-school sweetheart and she turned you down again?"

"I would have been humiliated."

"And you didn't love her enough to take that risk?"

"I—" He clamped his mouth shut. Poured the water into a teapot. "I was young."

"You do it with every woman you date. You pull back the instant you discover they don't value something the same as you."

"Because relationships need to be built on shared values. If Mom had loved living in the country, she wouldn't have run off for the glitz of the city."

"Maybe, but you don't fall in love with a checklist of ideals. You fall in love with a person, with all her faults and differing opinions—the way God made her. And you trust God to help you make it work, because relationships get messy no matter how many boxes on your checklist you've ticked."

"This from the woman who wears a wedding band to avoid being picked up by guys."

Her gaze dropped. She twisted the gold band.

"I'm sorry. I—"

"No, you're right. I have no business giving advice. But I still think you should go after her."

"She won't even open the door. What would you suggest? I ram it down?"

"What are you talking about? She's not home. Didn't you get the note she left?"

"Of course she's home. Her car's still in the driveway."

"That's because Neil drove her to the reception."

Josh's heart felt as if it'd been ripped from his chest. "Neil?"

Anne opened the front door and untaped a folded paper. "I'm sure she explained everything in this."

Josh glanced at his watch. Bec must've called Neil the second he'd left. "How could she go back to that creep after one little fight?"

"Why don't you go after her and find out?"

Josh unfolded the letter. His heart did a funny flip at the sight of a couple of tear-size wrinkles on the paper.

Dear Josh,
I wasn't sure if you'd still want to go on the tour with me so when Neil stopped by and offered to escort me, I agreed. We'll hitch rides on a few of the other cars tomorrow. Might add some diversity to my article.

"Might give her more opportunities to ferret out what people know about the jewelry theft," Josh muttered under his breath. She was too obstinate for her own good. He flipped through his address book and dialed the number for the tour's director.

"What are you doing?"

"Making sure word of the stolen jewelry's recovery gets spread. At least then Bec will be safe."

"You could go make sure of that yourself, you know."

"I think I can do without your advice. It was your ridiculous idea that got me entangled with Bec in the first place. I was perfectly happy being single."

"Liar."

Bec's betrayed expression flashed through his thoughts. Her crackly *I thought you were someone I could count on* echoed painfully in his ears. He'd let her down.

Sure, her idea had been irrational, but he could've discussed options with her. Maybe they could have found a way to use the jewelry to catch the guy.

"May I help you?" the tour director asked over the phone, jerking Josh from his thoughts.

"Uh, sorry, no. Wrong number."

Anne lifted an eyebrow as he hung up the phone.

"Don't gloat."

"I wouldn't dream of it."

"Being humiliated in front of a room full of strangers can't be any worse than spending the rest of my life wondering if I could have won her back."

"Let alone living without her."

"Yeah, that, too." Josh dashed to the bedroom and quickly changed back into his old-fashioned getup, then snatched up the keys to his truck. "Lock up, will you?" He jogged across the driveway to hook his truck back up to the trailer.

He stopped short at the sound of Bruiser barking.

Sarah's husband stood on the back porch, his hands cupped around his eyes, peering through the kitchen window.

"What are you doing?"

The man jolted back. "Looking for my wife. Have you seen her?"

Josh bristled at the thought of what he might've done to make her leave this time. "Not since the night she went home with you."

Rowan smoothed his expensive-looking suit and gave Josh's outfit a cursory once-over. "Do you know where Becki is?"

"Not at the moment. But I can let her know you're looking for her next time I see her."

Rowan gave one last glance over his shoulder at the kitchen window. "Don't worry about it, thanks." The man climbed into his car and hightailed it out of the driveway before Josh finished hooking on the trailer.

A few minutes later two police cruisers pulled in, followed

by Smith's Plymouth. Hunter jumped out of the first cruiser and strode toward Josh, a sober look on his face.

"What's wrong? Did something happen to Bec?"

Hunter flashed him the paper he was carrying. "We have a warrant to search the premises."

"For the other glove? I already told you she'll turn it in if she finds it." Josh snatched the warrant from Hunter's hand. "Please tell me you're not trying to pin this on the Graws."

A thump sounded at the porch door—Bruiser throwing himself at it, barking frantically.

"Can you tie the dog up at your house until we're done?" Hunter asked, confirming Josh's fear.

Henry Smith—the insurance company's private investigator—studied Josh for a full thirty seconds before speaking. "Where is Miss Graw?"

"Why? She has nothing to do with this."

"A missing fifty-thousand-dollar necklace and earring set say otherwise."

The instant Neil drew close to the parking lot of the Grand Hotel, Becki scanned the rows of cars for her sister's. She had no idea what Sarah's idea for catching the jewel thief was, but at this point she'd be happy just to find her sister was safe.

"You okay?" Neil turned his car into the lot. "You're trembling."

Becki curled her fingers into the small satin clutch she'd grabbed to go with the outfit. "I don't see my sister's car. She was supposed to meet me here."

"What kind of car?"

"A BMW, if…" Becki twisted in her seat and scrutinized each car they passed. Would Sarah have taken the BMW? With the built-in GPS, she'd be too easy to locate. "Um, actually, she probably came in a different car. Let's just go inside and see if we can find her."

Neil parked in a dark corner. "Stay put until I get your door."

She hung her camera strap over her shoulder and then placed her hand in his. She couldn't help but be impressed by his chivalry. "I appreciate your escorting me to this, Neil."

"It's my pleasure. Like old times."

Becki nodded, but as he cupped her elbow to guide her to the entrance, her insides didn't bubble as they did whenever Josh touched her. She shoved the thought from her mind. Her sister had just run away from an abusive husband. Did she need any more proof that a few momentary flutters weren't worth the inevitable heartache?

She breathed in the cool evening air. Once she saw Sarah for herself—safe—she'd be able to relax. They reached the sidewalk, and a car door slammed behind them. High heels click-clacked toward them.

Becki whirled toward the sound. "Sarah!" She pulled her sister into a fierce hug. "Are you okay? I couldn't get you on your cell phone."

Sarah gave Neil a surreptitious glance and whispered, "I had to ditch it so Rowan couldn't track me. I left the car parked at the bus station and put the phone on a bus headed for Thunder Bay."

Becki laughed and hugged her sister harder. "Brilliant. That will keep him busy."

"Shall we go in?" Neil put an arm around each of them and ushered them inside.

"Mmm." Sarah inhaled. "Enraptured for Him, isn't it?"

"That's what's different," Becki said. "I knew there was something."

"It's the male version of the perfume I gave you," he said, sounding smug.

Just inside the door, they stopped at the coat check and Neil lifted the wrap from Becki's shoulder, then helped Sarah with her coat. He caught the scarf along with the coat, revealing a stunning necklace.

"Whoa," Becki exclaimed. That must have set Rowan back a fortune.

Sarah snatched back the scarf and wrapped it around her neck, darting a furtive look at Becki.

She must plan to hock the piece to finance her escape. Becki squeezed Sarah's hand to assure her she understood. As Neil handed in the coats in exchange for coat-check stubs, Becki drew Sarah aside. "Are you okay?"

"I didn't steal it from you." Sarah sounded worried.

"Steal what?"

Big-band music drifted from the ballroom as couples jostled past them.

Sarah tugged Becki into a shadowed alcove, where she unwound her scarf and touched the teardrop pendant hanging from the center of a diamond-studded chain. "You don't recognize this?"

"Should I?"

Sarah blew out a breath. "It was in Gran's glove."

"What?" Her mind scrolled through the images in the jewelry-theft article.

"I didn't know it was there when I took the glove," Sarah said defensively. "I just…I… The glove smelled like Gran."

A lump rose to Becki's throat. Sarah missed Gran and Gramps as much as she did.

"When I left so quickly that night Rowan came, I just wanted to grab something that would remind me of her. I should have told you when I got home and found the necklace inside. I thought it was Gran's and I hoped you wouldn't miss it. Can you ever forgive me?"

"Yes, but—" Becki pulled the edges of the scarf back together and lowered her voice. "It's got to be one of the stolen pieces."

"Yes. I thought if I wore it, the thief might reveal himself."

"That's your idea?" With sudden, terrifying clarity, Becki realized why Josh had so adamantly nixed *her* idea to do basically the same thing.

Hadn't the trashed trailer been proof enough the guy had lost patience? Not to mention maybe even tampered with her brakes. Once he set eyes on the necklace, he'd go after it no matter the cost.

Neil approached with a smile. "Finished your powwow?"

"Could you give us one more minute?" Becki asked, appreciative of his sensitivity.

Women in evening gowns sauntered past, scarcely paying them any attention, but the gaze of every man seemed drawn to her beautiful sister.

"Why don't I get everyone some punch?" Neil suggested.

"That would be wonderful. Thank you," Sarah said.

Once Neil disappeared through the ballroom doors, Becki said, "I can't let you do this, Sarah. It's too dangerous."

"What are you talking about? How did you think you'd draw out the thief?"

"I don't know. I was frantic over finding those jewels in Gran's glove and desperate to prove she didn't take them. But I won't risk your safety to do that."

"But you'll risk yours?"

Becki let out a sigh.

Sarah's fingers gripped her scarf. "I want to do this for Gran and Gramps just as much as you do. This can work."

Becki envisioned the last time they'd conspired together—to get a puppy—and the disaster that had turned into. "I don't even know what we'd do if we came up with a suspect."

"You're here to do an article. Take photos of everyone who shows an interest in the jewelry, especially if they seem to watch my every move."

"That's half the guys here."

"So take down names on the pretense of it being for the

article. If they don't want you to use their pictures or names, that'd be all the more suspicious."

"But if this guy is here, he's going to look for any opportunity to steal the necklace."

"So we let him." Sarah hooked her arm through Becki's and led her into the ballroom.

Tables laden with cakes and pastries lined the walls. Couples milled about them.

"If the guy steals the necklace, we don't have to prove anything," Sarah went on. "Just call the police and they'll catch him in possession of the stolen goods."

Like you are now? Becki silenced the voice in her head. The voice that sounded too much like Josh. This could work. It had to work.

Sarah unwound the scarf and draped it across her shoulders. The lights from the chandeliers made the attached pendant glitter.

Lifting her camera, Becki took a few steps back. "That necklace is stunning," she gushed loud enough for others to hear, and then she snapped a couple of photos of Sarah hamming it up for the camera.

The ploy attracted the attention they'd hoped. Several couples meandered over and admired the pendant. Becki took their photos, too. Told them she was writing an article. She glanced around, wondering what had happened to Neil. She spotted him chatting with an older lady by the punch bowl.

He gave Becki a warm smile and, with a slight lift of his chin, mouthed, *Be right there.*

She tightened her grip on her camera. He was being so nice, but she didn't want him to think this changed her mind about *them.*

Sarah's sudden gasp snapped Becki's attention back to her sister. Sarah clutched her scarf at her throat, her panicked gaze colliding with Becki's. Lifting her camera, Becki whirled to capture the source of Sarah's panic.

Josh.

Becki's heart slammed into her ribs. He didn't look like a policeman in his breeches and suspenders and crisp white shirt topped with a cravat. He looked noble, honorable, almost like someone she might be able to reason with. But that didn't change the fact he was first and foremost a cop, and if he'd seen the stolen necklace, she was finished.

SIXTEEN

Josh couldn't take his eyes off Bec as she lowered her camera and offered him an awkward smile. Okay, so she wasn't wearing the dress he liked, but she looked stunning in red. At the sight of her bare neck, relief filled him that she hadn't come with the stolen necklace to hatch some harebrained plan to nab the real thief.

She scanned the ballroom, and her creamy shoulders relaxed when her gaze met Neil's over the punch bowl.

She couldn't be serious about Neil. Could she?

Josh forced his fingers to unclench. He'd seen the way she'd flinched the day Neil had shown up uninvited.

He frowned. But if she didn't come to catch the thief, why was she here with Neil and not him?

Neil weaved through the crowd toward her, carrying two glasses of punch. Apparently he was someone she could count on.

Maybe coming here had been a mistake.

Couples dotted the room, heads inclined toward each other, whispering, laughing, sharing secret smiles. The way Bec's grandparents had always been. How many times had he noticed their eyes meeting across a crowded room as they shared a smile?

He wanted that with Bec.

He wanted the house in the country, full of rescued strays

and four kids whose names all started with *J* and a little Becki.

His heart squeezed as he closed the distance between them.

He'd already defied his captain's orders by coming here. If he was going to crash and burn, he might as well go all out.

"You came," she said with a hint of uncertainty, but had he imagined the hint of pleasure, too?

He let his gaze caress her skin. "The red looks good on you."

"Doesn't it?" Neil said smugly, handing Bec a glass of punch. "It's my favorite color."

Josh stiffened.

Apology washed through Bec's eyes, but Josh didn't know how to interpret it.

Neil handed the second glass to another woman.

Josh did a double take. "Sarah? I didn't expect to find you here."

She clenched a scarf about her neck with a white-knuckled grip, but he didn't miss the bruise under her left jaw.

A surge of anger gripped him. "Have you finally left him?"

The grip on her scarf relaxed a little. "Yes."

"That explains why he was at Bec's house looking for you."

"Who? Your husband?" Neil interjected.

"Yes."

Sarah set her glass on a table and fussed with the scarf at the back of her neck, then caught Bec's hand between hers.

Bec's eyes widened as they seemed to telegraph silent messages as only siblings could.

"I need to go," Sarah whispered. "Rowan might have followed Josh here."

Seeing Bec's gaze drop to the scarf hiding her sister's bruises, Josh interjected, "Where will you go? We could help you find a safe place."

"I have one lined up. Thank you." She squeezed Bec's fisted hand for a long moment. "I'll call you soon."

Neil produced a coat-check stub from his pocket. "I'll walk you to your car." He touched Bec's shoulder. "I'll just be a minute."

Josh watched them leave. Begrudgingly, he had to concede that Neil seemed like a decent guy, but that didn't stop Josh from hoping that Sarah kept Neil chatting outside for a good long time.

As Josh turned back to Bec, she fumbled with her purse, sloshing punch over her gloved hand.

He lifted the glass from her hold. "It's stained."

"That's okay. It'll wash." She hurriedly snapped shut her tiny purse.

At the sight of a diamond-studded chain dangling from it, Josh's planned speech died on his lips.

Bec reached for her punch glass, but Josh caught her wrist. "Why did you come?"

"What do you mean? I'm here to write an article."

He set down the punch glass, opened her purse, nudged the chain inside—against his better judgment—and snapped the purse shut again. "I mean, you better let me in on whatever plan you've concocted."

"I didn't keep the necklace from you, Josh." He steeled himself against her defensive expression. "You have to believe me. Sarah had it. She didn't tell me until I got here."

"That's why you scrambled to hide it in your purse when I wasn't looking? When did I become the enemy?"

Her expression crumbled.

His anger seeped away. "I'm sorry, Bec." He stroked her cheek. "Trust me, if I didn't believe in you, I wouldn't be here. The police know about the missing jewelry."

Her face paled, and everything in him wanted her to believe he could help her, but he couldn't sugarcoat the truth. "You're their prime suspect."

* * *

"They think I stole it?" Clutching her purse, Becki searched Josh's eyes. He didn't think that, too, did he?

No, he'd said he believed in her.

Josh steered her away from the crowds into a quiet corner. "They think you *found* the jewelry, but *withheld* the necklace and earring set."

"But you know I wouldn't steal them. You told them. Didn't you?"

He looked pointedly at her purse.

"Sarah had the necklace. I didn't know."

"Bec, they found one of the earrings in your jewelry box, not to mention they know that Sarah threatened to oust you out of your house if you didn't give her a bigger cut of the inheritance."

"Fine, don't believe me. Take it."

Josh covered her hand and closed the clasp an instant before Neil's arm curled around her waist.

"Ready to hobnob?" Neil murmured close to her ear. "Get that story you're after?"

Josh's hand dropped to his side. Something flickered in his eyes. His expression went blank. "I need to make a phone call." Josh walked a few steps, then pivoted on his heel. "By the way, I towed the Model T here. We could ask Hunter's uncle if it'd be okay for you and Neil…"

He'd towed the car? Really?

"That'd be great. Don't you think?" Neil piped up.

"Yes." Becki turned back to her date and mustered a smile.

He'd towed the car? He didn't just come to recover the jewelry? How sweet was that? Had he hoped to join her, too?

"I thought your article might sound better from a front-seat view."

Her article. Right. He'd been rescuing her again.

If only her heart wouldn't somersault in her chest every

time Josh acted like some fairy-tale prince. She knew better than to believe in fairy tales.

What had she expected? That he'd turn into a green-eyed monster like her sister had supposed?

You actually had to love someone to be jealous.

Josh slammed his fist into the side of the trailer. God help him, when he saw Neil slink his arm around Bec's waist, and Bec not so much as lean away, his chest had felt as if she'd dug that old-fashioned boot heel square into the center.

He pulled out his phone and clicked Hunter's number.

"You got it?" Hunter asked the instant the phone connected.

"Soon." Josh sucked in the night air, but the heavy dampness did nothing to relieve the fire in his chest. "I'll need you to bring it in, though. I need to stay and watch Bec's back."

"Already on my way. Got Anne with me."

Josh stuffed the phone back in his pocket and sucked in a couple more deep breaths. He'd quietly corner Bec one last time, recover the necklace and then back off. Scan the crowd. Make sure no one was watching her.

He turned back to the hotel, but a faint whimper stopped him. He glanced around, expecting to find an abandoned kitten or pup. This end of the parking lot backed onto the cliff above the ravine and wasn't well lit—just the kind of place someone might choose to dump an unwanted pet.

The whimper sounded again—from the direction of the ravine. Josh reached into his truck and grabbed his flashlight. He swept the light over the steep embankment and caught sight of a blond head.

He scrambled toward the victim. "I'm coming. Hang on."

Six feet from the gagged, prone body, his heart slammed into his ribs. "Sarah?" *Oh, God, please let her be okay.*

A purple splotch colored her cheek. Her dress was torn and muddy. Leaves and twigs tangled her hair.

"Sarah? Sarah, can you hear me?"

Her eyes remained closed. Her face twisted in pain.

He skidded to his knees and untied the scarf binding her mouth. Guilt cut off his breath. He must have led Rowan straight to her. Josh checked her breathing, her pulse. "Sarah, talk to me." He unbound her hands; they'd been tied behind her back with the belt of her dress. It was a miracle she'd been conscious enough to make any sound after being pushed over the ravine with no hands to brace her fall.

He checked her arms and legs for fractures. They'd need a spinal board just to be safe. He pulled out his cell phone and dialed 9-1-1.

The phone flashed No Service. "Sarah, can you hear me? I need to climb up the ravine to get a signal so we can get you an ambulance."

Her eyelids fluttered open.

"Did you hear me? I'll be right back."

"Becki?" she whispered.

"In the hotel. I'll call her, too."

"No!" She struggled to get to a sitting position.

He gently urged her back down. "You need to lie still until the paramedics get here."

She lashed at his arms, her eyes flaring. "You have to protect her."

Josh cupped her shoulders. "It's okay. Rowan's not going to bother Bec in a ballroom full of people." His calm tone belied the frantic scramble in his chest. "Neil will watch out for her."

Sarah flailed out of his grasp. "No, not—" She pushed herself up and immediately blacked out.

"Sarah?" Josh shook her gently, terrified to move her.

Her breathing remained steady.

"I'll be right back." He raced up the steep incline, his gaze glued to his cell-phone screen. The instant a signal appeared, he called in an ambulance and police, then rushed back to Sarah's side.

She drifted in and out of consciousness, mumbling gibberish.

At the top of the ravine, a car door slammed.

"Hello, up there!" he shouted. "I need help."

"Josh?" Hunter's voice floated down the ravine.

Josh pointed his flashlight toward the ridge. "Down here. Bec's sister is injured."

Hunter and Anne plowed down the ravine toward them. Anne immediately began assessing Sarah's injuries. "What happened?"

"Her husband found her," Josh said flatly. He'd never forgive himself for leading the brute straight to her. "We need to put out a BOLO alert for him."

At the mention of a be-on-the-lookout, Sarah's eyes flew open. "No." She grabbed his arm when he reached to hold her still. "Not Rowan."

"What?" Josh turned the light to her face.

Her hand went to her throat. "He thought I still had the necklace."

"Who?" Josh surged to his feet, praying he wasn't too late to get to Bec.

Tears filled Sarah's eyes. "Neil."

SEVENTEEN

Josh raced back inside the hotel and then forced himself to slow his steps as he reached the entrance to the ballroom. He wanted to storm in, knock Neil's lights out for terrorizing Bec these past weeks and pull her safe into his arms. Instead, he stood in the doorway and methodically scanned the room.

If he played it cool, Neil wouldn't know he'd found Sarah and was onto him. Just like he hadn't known the jewelry had already been turned in.

Josh toed off the worst of the mud caked to his shoes.

A gray-haired lady looked over her glasses at him as she walked past.

A minute later, a hotel employee touched his shoulder, the nosy woman at the employee's flank. "May I help you, sir?"

Josh flashed his police ID. "I'm looking for Becki Graw. She was wearing a long red gown."

"The woman with the camera?" the gray-haired lady piped up.

"Yes. Have you seen her?"

"She and her husband left about half an hour ago. Probably went up to their rooms. I noticed because—"

"Can you give me her room number?" Josh asked the hotel employee. "We have reason to believe she might be in danger from the man she was with."

"Of course. Follow me." The employee hurried to the desk

and typed on the computer. "No, we have no one registered under that name."

"What about Neil Orner?"

The employee tapped a few more keys as unwelcome feelings crammed Josh's throat.

"No, sorry."

Josh peeled a business card out of his wallet. "Check the security cameras, bathrooms, everywhere. If you see the woman, call me immediately."

His cell phone rang before he made it out the door. Josh checked the screen. Hunter.

"Anne went to the hospital with Sarah. Neil ransacked her car, too."

Josh hit the door at a run. "We're looking for a red Mustang. Someone saw Bec leave with Neil a half hour ago."

"On it."

Josh raced up one row of cars and down the other. If only he hadn't walked out on Bec back at the house, she never would have gone off with Neil. Josh reached the back corner of the lot at the same time as Hunter.

"It's not here!" Dread cut off his breath.

"I put out a BOLO alert with both the local and highway police," Hunter said. "Sarah said Neil was ranting that he'd lost his job and his house because of them."

"That's crazy. How's he figure?"

"Don't know about the job, but sounds like he was investing on margin and got caught short. Must've been counting on selling the jewelry to cover the margin call."

Josh climbed into his truck. "Then he's got to be headed for Serenity to get the rest of the jewelry."

"She would have told him he's too late."

"Not Bec. She'd know she had to buy time." Josh prayed he was right. He smacked his portable light onto his roof. Neil must've showed up at the house ready to demand the jewelry, only Bec surprised him by inviting him on the tour. Maybe gave him hope that he could win her back, or at least that he could get the jewelry without her learning the truth about him.

Hunter jogged to his truck. "I'll call the captain. Tell him to have someone watch the house."

Josh barreled out of the parking lot and floored the gas with Hunter on his tail. *Please, Lord, let our guess be right.* Neil had already lost his job, his house and his girl. He had nothing left to lose. If he couldn't get away with the jewelry, there was no telling what he'd do.

Eyes closed, Becki smacked her tongue against the roof of her mouth, trying to draw moisture to take away the strange taste. Her seat bounced, jostling her. Where was she?

She tried to open her eyes, but she couldn't seem to make her eyelids cooperate. The whir of an engine filtered through her thoughts. She was in a car?

She couldn't remember leaving the reception.

She turned her face toward the driver and this time managed to pry open her eyes.

Neil glanced from the road to her and smiled. "Have a good sleep?"

She blinked, straining to make sense of how she'd gotten here. Her mind flailed back over the evening. She remembered Josh leaving the reception to make a phone call. After that, things got fuzzy.

"I knew if I was patient you'd realize we were meant to be together."

What? If he thought they were a couple again, he'd totally misinterpreted her invitation to the reception.

Wait. Her sister. He'd said they had to hurry, that her sister needed her. Only… She pressed her fingers to her temples, straining to remember what he'd said.

Images flashed through her mind. She'd been about to climb into his car when she'd heard Josh shout from the direction of the ravine.

"You don't want him," Neil had snarled into her ear as he clamped a cloth over her mouth and nose, and her mind drifted into oblivion.

"After we pick up the rest of the jewelry, I was thinking we could fly to the Caribbean," Neil said. "What do you think?"

The jewelry? He knew about that? She felt in her lap for her purse.

He patted his pocket. "Don't worry. The necklace is safe and sound."

"That's all there is. My gran never had—"

Neil cackled. "You and I both know that necklace wasn't your grandmother's."

"But…how do you know that?"

His grin chilled her to the bone. "Because I took them."

"You?"

"Is that so hard to believe? I have many talents. I could have made you a wealthy woman."

"I—" She caught herself before saying she didn't care about money. "I've always wanted to go to the Caribbean," she mumbled instead, hoping that playing along with his delusion would buy her time.

He turned his car onto her road, cruising slowly past her house.

"Where are you going? You passed—"

He pulled into the rutted farm lane behind her property. "My parking spot." He threw her another creepy grin.

It was now or never. She quietly unfastened her seat belt and sprang out the door. Hiking up her long gown, she sprinted for the trees, remembering too late that her ankle couldn't handle the strain.

He tackled her, and she pitched face-first into the dirt.

"I should have known you were lying." He wrenched her arms behind her back and cinched them with a zip tie until the plastic dug into her wrists. She'd never be able to outrun him now.

She rolled onto her back and struggled to get up, refusing to ask for help. She wouldn't give him the satisfaction.

He hauled her to her feet. Snatched her purse from the front seat of the car, extracted her key and jabbed it at her face. "We can do this the easy way or the hard way."

"I don't know where the rest of the jewelry is," Becki yelled, hoping against hope that someone would hear her and send help.

"Don't lie to me. I saw the earring, remember?" Neil's grip tightened painfully around her arm. "I don't want to hurt you, Rebecca, but if you don't start telling me what I want to know, you'll be joining your sister."

"What did you do to her?" Sarah couldn't be dead. *Please, Lord, I won't believe it.*

Neil shoved her ahead of him through the damp meadow that backed onto her house. Josh's yard light scarcely cut through the thick darkness of the moonless night. But Neil moved confidently, as if he'd been that way before.

Just as Josh had first suspected. Why hadn't she listened?

As they got closer, the familiar shape of her grandparents' house emerged. A smidgen of hope surged through her.

Somehow she had to stall Neil, buy time until Josh figured out where she'd been taken.

Thank God she didn't tell Neil that the rest of the jewelry had already been turned in. If he killed her sister—*please, Lord, don't let that be true*—he wouldn't hesitate to finish her off, too.

A car rolled slowly up the road. Neil slapped his clammy hand over her mouth and clamped his other arm around her waist, drawing her tight against his chest, and hauled her to a stop.

As the car drew close, Becki could just make out the outline of something on its roof. *A patrol car!*

She struggled against Neil's grip, praying the officer would spot her. Had Josh sent him? She knew she could count on him.

The patrol car turned into her driveway and two officers got out.

Neil's arm snaked from her waist to her neck and squeezed. The air stalled in her chest, flaming through her throat. Searing pain shot to her head, and what little she could see began to fade. "I don't need you alive to search that house, Rebecca," Neil hissed into her ear.

She stopped fighting, and his hold loosened a fraction.

She sucked in a lungful of air. *Oh, God, he's going to kill me.*

The officers shone their flashlights around the yard, peered through the windows, checked the barn.

Neil drew her deeper into the shadows.

"Let's go," one of the officers said, turning back to the car. "There's nobody here."

Becki lurched forward and tried to shout, but with Neil's hand clamped over her mouth, she barely managed a squeak and a scuffle.

The second officer turned his flashlight in their direction.

Neil pinned her against his chest.

The light beam scraped the ground yards from their feet, then abruptly spiraled toward the driveway.

The officers climbed back into the car and slammed the doors.

"Serenity's finest at work," Neil said with a sneer. "Your new boyfriend won't come to your rescue this time. Trust me. Guys don't like to be snubbed for another man."

"Why are you doing this?" she mumbled through his fingers.

"I need the money. Why else?"

The patrol car backed slowly down the driveway and kept on going.

No! Come back! the voice in her head screamed.

"Move," Neil snarled, shoving her forward again. "This is your fault. If you hadn't broken up with me when I got back from the car tour, we would have paid your grandparents a nice friendly visit. I would have recovered my jewelry from the hiding place in your grandfather's car. And no one would have been the wiser."

"You were on that tour?"

He laughed. "It would've been perfect. If they hadn't croaked." Another set of headlights turned onto the road.

Neil dragged her into the shadow of the barn and crouched low.

She couldn't see the car, but its headlights draped the far-off trees in a ghostly light.

Neil's back teeth clicked in the familiar rat-a-tat that meant he was growing impatient.

Finally the car passed and disappeared down the road.

"C'mon." Neil pushed her toward the house.

She dug in her heels. "But you said the jewelry was in the car."

"Nice try. I already checked."

"You're the one that clobbered me over the head my first night here?"

"I couldn't afford to let you see me." His foot kicked something, sent it rattling against the barn wall. "What the—" He flicked his flashlight toward the sound.

The gasoline can. Josh must've left it out after he topped up the car.

Neil picked up the can and shook it. Gasoline sloshed. "This could come in handy. Maybe you'll start talking if I threaten to burn down your beloved house, room by room, eh?"

"No, please."

"Begging doesn't become you." He shoved her up the back steps.

She stepped on the hem of her gown and pitched to her knees.

He grabbed her arm and lifted her back to her feet, causing the bottom of her gown to rip. "Move." He jostled the can of gasoline tauntingly.

Her legs moved woodenly. *Think.* She had to stall him. "So you put that note in my mailbox, too," she asked loudly, hoping to alert Bruiser.

"Yup."

"And the sulfur in my well?"

"Sulfur? No, can't take credit for that."

"But you made those phone calls and tampered with the brakes and shot at the house?"

"The potshots were inspired, don't you think? Made it look like an incompetent hunter to show you how dangerous country living was. Too bad you didn't take the hint."

"So I'd come back to you?"

"I figured you'd see the light sooner or later. How long could a neighbor-farmer boy keep a sophisticated woman like you entertained?" Neil peered through the window on the kitchen door. "Where's your dog?"

Becki looked, too. There was no sign of him. "I don't know."

Neil tapped the door.

Still no barking.

Becki's hope drained. Josh had said the police had searched her house. He must've taken Bruiser away.

Neil unlocked the kitchen door and pushed her inside.

Automatically she hitched up her elbow to flick on the light switch.

He slapped it off. "Nice try." The dead bolt clicked with a sickening ping. Then he caught her by the chin and pushed her up until she was standing on her tiptoes, back pressed to the wall. "Try anything like that again and you'll regret it." In the dim light seeping through the windows, he studied her face for a long moment, pressing her head harder against the wall. His thumb licked across her bottom lip.

Closing her eyes, she sucked in a breath. *Please, Lord, don't let him hurt me.*

As suddenly as he'd grabbed her, he flung her away. "We could have been good together."

She scanned the room for a weapon, struggling to regain her balance. There were plenty of knives, but with her hands tied behind her back, how would she use one?

Neil snapped down the kitchen blinds, then stalked into the living room and drew the drapes. Utter darkness swallowed her.

Darkness is as light to God. Her Gran's words whispered through her mind. She began to make out shapes in the room. She knew every inch of this house in the dark or light. If she could just free her hands…

Neil disappeared down the hallway, followed by the sound of more blinds snapped shut. Did he plan to turn on the lights?

Or was he afraid she would?

She twisted her hands within her binds, straining to pull free. But she could scarcely move, let alone manipulate the tie with her numb fingers. She plowed backward until she slammed into the wall, then felt her way toward the door. Her fingers contacted the cool metal of the doorknob, and she inched them higher toward the dead bolt.

A light suddenly flashed into her eyes. "Where do you think you're going?" Neil's long strides swallowed the distance between them. He grabbed a hunk of her hair.

Pain screamed through her scalp.

He pushed her toward the living room. "You love this house. Isn't that what you told me?"

He let out an icy chuckle, punctuated by the slosh of gasoline.

A chill shivered down her arms.

"If you don't produce the rest of my jewelry, your stay will be permanent."

EIGHTEEN

Josh pulled up to the makeshift command post behind Bec's house, where Serenity police had found Neil's car. "See anything?" He yanked off his white shirt and tugged on a spare black T-shirt.

Wes handed him a Kevlar vest, then held up a stained white glove. "Found this on the floor of the car. Recognize it?"

"Yeah." Heart racing, Josh thumbed through his keys for the one to the lockbox bolted to his truck floor.

"There are no lights on in the house. How do you want to play this?"

Play this? This wasn't a war game. This was Bec's life. "We'll scout the situation first."

"The tactical team's on its way."

Yeah, he wouldn't be waiting. He pulled out his gun and loaded a clip.

Hunter strode up, already outfitted in full tactical gear. He handed Josh a black paint pot and night-vision goggles. "Just saw a flash of light in the second-story window, west wall, second from the back."

"Does this guy own a gun?" Wes asked.

"I don't know." Josh fitted an earpiece and mic and lowered his goggles. "Let's go."

He and Hunter stole across the field in silence, an exercise they'd done countless times during night ops the three years they'd served together in the military. But Josh's gut had never felt as strangled as it did tonight.

At the edge of the yard, he motioned for Hunter to take the front. Within minutes, Hunter's whispered voice sounded through the earpiece.

"Can't get a visual."

"Same here. Doors and windows are locked."

A scrap of fabric fluttered past his foot.

Josh stooped to pick it up, recognized the silky feel of the dress Bec had worn tonight. *She's here.*

"A light just went on in a second-story window, back of house, west end," an officer's voice said over the mic.

Josh glanced at the barn. "Get a sniper in the hayloft."

"I'll go." Hunter said. "Think you can get in through the basement without him hearing you?"

"I can do better than that." Josh pulled out the spare key Bec had given him. "You in position?"

"Just about."

Josh listened at the door, then fit in the key. "Command post, on Hunter's mark, make the call. Patch it to our comms. I want to know what this guy's saying." Josh inched open the door, scanned the area. The green, filmy image through his goggles betrayed no movement. He entered. "I'm in," he whispered.

The smell of gasoline assaulted him. "Get the fire department here," he growled into his mic. "He's gonna torch the place!"

"In position," Hunter said.

"Backup standing by," command post announced. "Putting in the call now."

Josh quickly checked the main-floor rooms. Strewn clothes and books littered the floor.

The house phone rang once. Twice.

Come on, pick up. Josh stole up the stairs.

The ringing stopped. Josh inched toward the bedroom

door. What was going on? He tapped his earpiece. Had Neil picked up or not?

"This is Officer Wade of the Serenity Police Department" Josh heard through the comm.

No response.

Back pressed to the wall outside the occupied room, Josh drew in a breath and shot a glance inside.

His heart lurched. Bec stood at the window, gasoline dripping from her hair, down her neck and over her gown in black, angry rivulets.

Josh jerked back out of sight. "You don't have a clear shot," he hissed into the mic. "I repeat—"

"Copy that," Hunter responded, and Josh's breath left him in a rush.

"Mr. Orner, we know you're holding Miss Graw against her will. Let her go and come out with your hands up."

"Rebecca is exactly where she wants to be. In her beloved home," Neil said in an icy voice and slammed down the phone.

Josh took another peek, and Bec's gaze shot in his direction.

Her eyes went soft, brimming with emotion he'd thought he'd never see again.

He touched a silencing finger to his lips.

She shifted her eyes to the left and back.

He nodded and moved to the other side of the door to get into a position where he could see Neil. He jerked back at the sight of his own reflection in the dresser mirror.

Neil caught Bec by the hair. "So your boyfriend found you after all."

Josh's hands went slick with sweat. He was 99 percent sure Neil hadn't seen him, that he was referring to the phone call.

Neil lifted an old silver lighter to Bec's face. "Think he'll still want you after the flames are through with you?" His thumb flipped back the lid and caressed the lighter's igniter.

The terror in Bec's eyes shredded Josh's heart. Somehow he had to distract Neil enough to ease his grip.

Fire engine sirens split the air.

Neil's thumb turned jerky on the lighter. "I'm not going to jail. I'd sooner burn with you in hell."

"Kill the sirens," Josh hissed into his mic. "He's antsy enough."

As if Bec knew exactly what Josh needed her to do, she edged out of his line of fire.

Neil yanked her to his chest. "What are you doing?"

Her gaze lifted to the opposite wall, and the terror slipped from her eyes. "I was trying to see the picture of Jesus better."

"He's not going to save you." Neil clamped his arm around Bec's waist, holding her like a shield. "Neither is that boyfriend of yours. You want out of this alive—" Neil swiveled her away from the painting "—you do exactly as I say."

Bec dug in her heels. "Wait. I don't want you hurt, either."

"Call him again," Josh whispered into his mic. "Hunter, get ready to take the shot on my signal."

The phone rang.

Neil ignored it. "You don't love me," he growled. "So don't bother pretending."

"I may not love you the way you'd hoped," Bec said, her voice surprisingly calm. "But I care about you. And Jesus—"

"*Care* about me?" Neil roared and took a wild swing at the blaring phone.

Josh barreled into the room, scooped Bec from Neil's arm and dived into a roll. "Now. Now. *Now,*" he yelled.

Three shots cracked through the glass and blinds.

"No!" Bec screamed.

Neil clapped a hand to his chest, shock glazing his eyes.

Josh hoisted Bec to her feet and pushed her toward the door, wrists still bound. "Get out."

His backup charged up the stairs as Neil lifted the lighter. "Get her out of here," Josh ordered.

Neil's gaze fixed on Josh, pure hatred blazing from his eyes.

"Let me help you," Josh soothed, taking a cautious step forward.

Neil flicked on the lighter, an ugly sneer curling his lips.

The lighter tumbled to the floor.

A roar shook the house. Flames shot out the bedroom door, blasting Josh's backup off their feet.

"Josh!" Becki screamed from the base of the stairs.

Hunter hoisted her over his shoulder and hustled her out the front door.

Firemen dragging hoses streamed toward the house.

"We have two men down at the top of the stairs. Two men in the second bedroom on the right," Hunter reported to the chief, setting her down on the back of the ambulance.

The paramedic snipped the binds cinching her wrists. Becki sprang from the ambulance.

Hunter caught her.

She thrashed her arms. "Let me go. Josh is in there. This is my fault."

Hunter tightened his hold, lifting her off the ground.

She kicked wildly.

He gave her a hard shake. "Racing back in there isn't going to help. Stay here and let the firefighters do their job."

Two firefighters came out the front door, each helping a hacking, smoke-blackened tactical officer.

She strained against Hunter's hold, needing to go to Josh the second he appeared.

But he didn't.

She watched in horror as flames melted through the second-story window blinds and yellow-brown smoke puffed from the eaves. A couple of firefighters hauled a chain saw up a ladder.

"What are they doing? Why aren't they going after Josh?" She clutched Hunter's arm. "They can't let him die."

"They're cutting a ventilation hole to lift the smoke off the guys inside." He set her back on the end of the ambulance. "Wait here," he ordered and strode to the rescued officers. Hunter spoke in low whispers.

The other officer shook his head.

No! Lord, please, You can't let him die.

Her lungs felt raw from the smoke filling the air. Neil's taunts echoed in her mind. His sick pleasure in dousing her precious home with gasoline, in telling her how it would burn.

Yet, in that moment, all she'd cared about was believing her sister was still alive and seeing Josh again, telling him she was sorry.

Then when he found her and looked at her with such, such...*love,* she couldn't remember why she'd ever gotten angry with him. She loved him so much it hurt.

He hadn't returned the jewelry because he was a control freak like her brother-in-law or because he cared more about his job than her. He did it because he wanted her safe, because he was honorable, trustworthy, because he could be counted on. And she never got the chance to tell him.

Tears coursed down her cheeks.

"Hey," Hunter said. "We're going to get him out."

She nodded, willing herself to believe it, feeling a little of the peace seep back into her soul that she'd felt when she'd looked at that painting in the bedroom of Jesus cradling the lamb. She swiped at her cheeks with the back of her hand. "What about my sister? Neil said—" She choked on the memory.

"She's okay." Hunter squeezed her shoulder. "Neil beat her up pretty bad, but your sister is one tough lady. She'll be okay."

Two paramedics raced to the back of the house, pushing a gurney.

Becki cupped a hand over her mouth, afraid to hope. What if Josh...died? Could she still believe God cared then?

Josh's words whispered through her mind. *I focus on the things that show me He does.*

She closed her eyes, shutting out the image of her grandparents' home burning. *He saved my sister. He brought Josh in time to save me. He showed me what real love looks like. "Greater love has no man than this, that he lay down his life for his friends."*

The Bible verse she'd memorized as a little girl in Sunday School, and never really understood until today, scrolled through her mind. *I'll believe, Lord. No matter what.*

She sensed Hunter moving away and opened her eyes.

He had a finger pressed to his ear, listening intently. "Copy that," he said, his expression grim.

The paramedics reappeared, pushing the gurney more slowly this time.

Becki's throat thickened, her feet glued to the ground, her heartbeat reeling. A blanket covered the body on the gurney, including...his face. "Please, God, no." Tremors overtook her.

Hunter's warm hand came to rest on her shoulder. "Neil's choices led to his death, Bec. Not yours."

"Neil?" Becki swallowed the sudden relief that bubbled up from her chest. She didn't want Neil's life to end this way, either. But if that wasn't Josh...

Too scared to ask after him, she mutely watched the paramedics load Neil's body onto an ambulance and drive away. No sirens. No hurry. It was too late.

Hunter nudged her arm and pointed to the house.

Firemen surrounded it, anchored by hoses aimed at the upper story. The front door still sat open.

Then, at the side of the house, she saw him.

She picked up her skirt and ran into his arms.

He caught her in a bear hug. "Glad to see you, too," his voice rumbled close to her ear, husky with emotion or maybe from the smoke.

She wrapped her arms around his waist and hugged him as if there was no tomorrow. "I'm sorry. I—"

Josh nudged her head up from his chest and stroked the hair from her face.

She swallowed, her heart tumbling into the depths of his tender gaze. Soot and black paint smeared his face, but he'd never looked better.

He kissed her forehead, her temple, the tip of her nose, her cheek and finally her lips.

Savoring the sweet taste of reunion, she returned his kiss, pouring out her love for him. Finally, she touched her forehead to his. "I came here hoping to find peace in the home I'd once loved so dear. I never—"

Josh released a ragged sigh. "I'm sorry we couldn't save it, Bec. I know how much—"

She touched a finger to his lips. "You didn't let me finish." She nestled into his arms. "This is home."

EPILOGUE

On a sunny May evening, standing in a tux at the front of the church, Josh clasped Bec's hands in his and said the words he'd been longing to pronounce for ten long months. "I do."

Bec's smile widened, and his heart expanded with sheer joy.

He swept the filmy white veil from her shoulders and cradled her face in his hands, soaking in the promise of forever beaming from Bec's eyes. He lowered his head and...

"Ahem." The pastor cleared his throat. "I haven't gotten to that part yet."

The congregation tittered, and Josh looked up with a sheepish grin.

The pastor winked and resumed, "I now pronounce you man and wife." He paused dramatically. "You may *now* kiss the bride."

"Finally," Josh said, and he did just that, smiling against his bride's lips as thunderous applause mingled with laughter broke out.

Josh eased back with a contented sigh. "I love you, Mrs. Rayne."

"I love you, too," she whispered.

Josh curled her hand through the crook of his arm and turned her to the still-applauding guests. And sitting beside his sister, with tears streaming down her face, his mom applauded loudest of all.

As he led Bec up the aisle, his heart raced with anticipation, and a little trepidation, over the surprise waiting for her outside—her grandfather's Cadillac restored.

Of course, the surprise paled in comparison to the gift she'd given him last night—suggesting that, instead of rebuilding the farmhouse and selling one of their places, they combine the land...if he still wanted to farm. And maybe use the house settlement to buy back what his dad had sold off, too.

Standing at the back of the church, Mrs. O'Reilly winked at him.

The church doors opened to an honor guard of saluting officers.

Taken up by the display, Bec didn't seem to notice the officer at the curb opening the Cadillac's back door.

Josh gave her a nudge and tilted his head toward the street.

Her look of absolute delight calmed his runaway heartbeat. "Oh, Josh. It's just like Gramps and Gran's. Wherever did you hire it?" Sudden moisture glistened in her eyes.

He squeezed her hand, certain she was wishing they could have shared this day.

"Hire it?" Hunter razzed from directly behind them, already tugging at his bow tie. "He worked us like slaves. Didn't pay us a penny."

"Worked you?" Bec's forehead crinkled adorably. "That's... Gramps's car?"

Josh nodded.

"But...I don't understand. The lawyer said the insurance company wrote it off after he convinced them to pay a settlement. Did—" Bec's gaze jerked to her matron-of-honor sister. "Did you put the money I gave you into the car?"

"No, I'm as surprised as you."

No doubt Sarah had been too preoccupied with the intensive counseling she and her husband had recently started after their lengthy separation. "It's your wedding present from me," Josh explained. "I bought it at scrap value and wangled the guys into helping me repair it."

"Oh, Josh!" Bec threw her arms around his neck. "I love it. Thank you."

Curling his arms around her waist and inhaling her sweet scent, his heart soared. "And how does a cross-country tour sound for our honeymoon?"

She pulled away just enough to meet his gaze, her expression suddenly serious. "Do you promise to check the cotter pins before we set out each day?"

"Without fail."

Her lips spread into a smile more radiant than the deepening colors of the setting sun. "Then I say it sounds like a wonderful adventure."

Josh dipped his head and whispered against her lips, "Every day with you is sure to be an adventure."

"Are you saying I'm trouble, Joshua Rayne?" she said teasingly.

"With a capital *T,* Mrs. Rayne. With a capital *T.*"

* * * * *

Dear Reader,

Writing this story turned into an unforeseen challenge as the characters veered into uncharted detours and threw roadblocks in my path. I hope you enjoyed a few surprises yourself. I had a lot of fun researching antique cars and car clubs for this story, but, regrettably, could include only a few of the many fascinating details I learned. "Horseless carriage" tours sound like wonderful adventures—worth exploring if you ever have the chance.

I'd love to hear about your own exploits. You can reach me via email at SandraOrchard@ymail.com or on Facebook at http://www.facebook.com/SandraOrchard. To learn about upcoming books and read interesting bonus features, please visit me online at www.SandraOrchard.com and sign up for my newsletter for exclusive subscriber giveaways.

Sincerely,
Sandra Orchard

Questions for Discussion

1. Josh gave up his dream of becoming a farmer, but he wasn't willing to give up making his home on the family farm, even for the love of a woman. What dreams would you give up for love?

2. After losing her grandparents, Becki grows to realize that she'd never owned her grandparents' faith for herself. Are you living on borrowed faith?

3. Josh believes that not chasing after a woman who leaves shows respect for her choice, whereas his sister suggests that the woman might really want him to come after her. Have you ever kept to yourself what you'd like a loved one to do to show his or her love? Did you hope he or she would just figure it out?

4. Becki begins to feel that God is asking her to give up her grandparents' home so she can help her sister. Have you ever felt God nudging you to give something up for another? What did you do?

5. Josh's faith is strong, yet he struggles to trust God in his relationships. Instead he's established a mental checklist of criteria a woman must meet, a checklist that keeps him from risking his heart. Is there an area of your life that you're resistant to surrender to God?

6. Becki's sister didn't want Becki to know that her husband was abusive. Do you think she was prompted by shame, embarrassment, pride or a desire to protect Becki? What might prompt you to keep something from a loved one?

7. To Josh's dismay, his friend Hunter has a tendency to speak before thinking. Does this happen to you? How might you curb the problem?

8. When Becki first arrives at her grandparents' house, happy memories flood her mind. What kind of memories are you creating with your loved ones?

9. Seeing Becki in Josh's arms fuels Neil's jealousy. He resists accepting her decision to leave him, the city, her job. Becki blames his controlling nature on his being bullied as a youth. Do you unconsciously try to overcome a deep-rooted wound in ways that might have unwelcome consequences?

10. Sunsets reminded Becki's grandmother that God is working behind the scenes even when we can't always see how. Similarly, when Becki asks Josh how he can keep believing God cares when things go bad, he responds that he looks for the good in his circumstances. Are you facing difficult circumstances? What good might come from them?

11. As welcoming as Joshua's protective arms feel, it's important to Becki that Josh see her as a woman who can take care of herself. Are you the kind of person who prefers to look out for yourself, or do you appreciate someone looking out for you?

12. Scents are powerful memory triggers for Becki. Are there any scents that stir strong memories in you?

REQUEST YOUR FREE BOOKS!

2 FREE RIVETING INSPIRATIONAL NOVELS
PLUS 2 FREE MYSTERY GIFTS

Love Inspired®
SUSPENSE

YES! Please send me 2 FREE Love Inspired® Suspense novels and my 2 FREE mystery gifts (gifts are worth about $10). After receiving them, if I don't wish to receive any more books, I can return the shipping statement marked "cancel." If I don't cancel, I will receive 4 brand-new novels every month and be billed just $4.74 per book in the U.S. or $5.24 per book in Canada. That's a savings of at least 21% off the cover price. It's quite a bargain! Shipping and handling is just 50¢ per book in the U.S. and 75¢ per book in Canada.* I understand that accepting the 2 free books and gifts places me under no obligation to buy anything. I can always return a shipment and cancel at any time. Even if I never buy another book, the two free books and gifts are mine to keep forever.

123/323 IDN F5AC

Name	(PLEASE PRINT)	
Address		Apt. #
City	State/Prov.	Zip/Postal Code

Signature (if under 18, a parent or guardian must sign)

Mail to the Harlequin® Reader Service:
IN U.S.A.: P.O. Box 1867, Buffalo, NY 14240-1867
IN CANADA: P.O. Box 609, Fort Erie, Ontario L2A 5X3

**Are you a current subscriber to Love Inspired Suspense books
and want to receive the larger-print edition?
Call 1-800-873-8635 or visit www.ReaderService.com.**

* Terms and prices subject to change without notice. Prices do not include applicable taxes. Sales tax applicable in N.Y. Canadian residents will be charged applicable taxes. Offer not valid in Quebec. This offer is limited to one order per household. Not valid for current subscribers to Love Inspired Suspense books. All orders subject to credit approval. Credit or debit balances in a customer's account(s) may be offset by any other outstanding balance owed by or to the customer. Please allow 4 to 6 weeks for delivery. Offer available while quantities last.

Your Privacy—The Harlequin® Reader Service is committed to protecting your privacy. Our Privacy Policy is available online at www.ReaderService.com or upon request from the Harlequin Reader Service.
We make a portion of our mailing list available to reputable third parties that offer products we believe may interest you. If you prefer that we not exchange your name with third parties, or if you wish to clarify or modify your communication preferences, please visit us at www.ReaderService.com/consumerschoice or write to us at Harlequin Reader Service Preference Service, P.O. Box 9062, Buffalo, NY 14269. Include your complete name and address.

LIS13R

Love Inspired
SUSPENSE
RIVETING INSPIRATIONAL ROMANCE

SEAL UNDER SIEGE
by
LIZ JOHNSON

Navy SEAL Tristan Sawyer rescued Staci Hayes, but the
missionary still isn't safe. With the bombing plot she overheard,
she and Tristan race to stop the terrorists before the naval base
goes up in smoke.

MEN OF VALOR

Available September 2013
wherever Love Inspired Suspense books are sold.